Undercover Angel

Dyan Sheldon is an award-winning children's author, adult novelist and humorist. Her titles include *Confessions of a Teenage Drama Queen* – now a major Hollywood film starring Lindsay Lohan and Adam Garcia – and its sequel, *My Perfect Life*; *Undercover Angel* and its sequel, *Undercover Angel Strikes Again*; *Sophie Pitt-Turnbull Discovers America*; *The Boy of My Dreams*; *Planet Janet* and its sequel, *Planet Janet in Orbit*; *And Baby Makes Two*; *Ride On, Sister Vincent*; and *Tall, Thin and Blonde*. She has also written books for younger children, including *Elena the Frog*; *He's Not My Dog*; *Leon Loves Bugs*; and the *Lizzie and Charley* series. American by birth, Dyan lives in north London.

Books by the same author

Elena the Frog
He's Not My Dog
Leon Loves Bugs
Lizzie and Charley Go Shopping
Lizzie and Charley Go to the Movies
Lizzie and Charley Go Away for the Weekend
Ride On, Sister Vincent
Undercover Angel Strikes Again

For older readers

And Baby Makes Two
The Boy of My Dreams
Confessions of a Teenage Drama Queen
My Perfect Life
Planet Janet
Planet Janet in Orbit
Sophie Pitt-Turnbull Discovers America
Tall, Thin and Blonde

Undercover Angel

DYAN SHELDON

WALKER BOOKS
AND SUBSIDIARIES
LONDON • BOSTON • SYDNEY • AUCKLAND

First published 2000 by Walker Books Ltd
87 Vauxhall Walk, London SE11 5HJ

This edition published 2004

2 4 6 8 10 9 7 5 3 1

This book has been typeset in Sabon

Printed in Great Britain by Cox & Wyman Ltd, Reading, Berkshire

British Library Cataloguing in Publication Data:
a catalogue record for this book is
available from the British Library

ISBN 1-84428-654-1

www.walkerbooks.co.uk

CONTENTS

THE NEW KID ARRIVES AND I FALL OFF THE ROOF

My name is Elmo Blue. My story sort of begins on the day I fell off the roof. It sort of begins on the day I fell off the roof, because that's the day the Bambers, who live across the road, brought the new kid home. And that's when everything started to happen. But technically my story begins the spring before, when my mother declared war on Mr Bamber.

I suppose I'd better explain.

My mother is what she calls an "environmental activist", which means she's always plodding through the rain with petitions or placards, trying to stop some road being built or some bird from losing its nesting ground. Among other things, Mr Bamber is a developer. Being a developer means that he's always trying to put in a new road or build a block of flats over some bird's nesting ground. Mr Bamber doesn't call my mother an "environmental activist". Mr Bamber calls my mother a "bleeding-heart pain-in-the-bum". When he isn't calling her "the green menace" or "our local representative of the lunatic fringe".

Last spring my mother discovered that Mr Bamber, who owned a great deal of land around Campton, was planning to level some nearby woods, dig up a couple of fields, move the old graveyard, drain the lake, and build a private estate with a pool and tennis courts and a golf club and stuff like that. The estate was going to be called Crosswoods Cove, even though Mr Bamber was destroying the woods and we weren't anywhere near the sea.

My mother went mad. She marched across the road to where Mr and Mrs Bamber were just getting into their car, and she told Mr Bamber that, as Chairman of the local chapter of Keep Our Planet Green, she was going to do everything in her power to stop his plans.

That was the first time I heard Mr Bamber call my mother a "bleeding-heart pain-in-the-bum".

"I've had enough of you and your kind, you bleeding-heart pain-in-the-bum!" boomed Mr Bamber. "And if you think I'm frightened of you and your petitions you're sadly mistaken." He laughed. "You and your pack of lunatic vegetarians are a thing of the past," Mr Bamber informed my mother. "You're stickin-the-mud old fogies. Man's about to colonize outer space, and you're worried about a couple of trees. Wake up and smell the coffee, Mrs Blue. Your day is over. You don't stand a chance."

My mother said, "We'll see about that," and marched back home.

My parents and Mr and Mrs Bamber were never friends. They were friendly when the Bambers first moved in, but they were too different to ever be friends. The Bambers are like a couple in a television advert – you know, normal – and my parents aren't. But they used to nod and smile when they saw one another, and I used to walk the Bambers' pit bull, Gregory, after school and at weekends. I liked walking Gregory. He's strong, but Mr Bamber had him specially trained to be a guard dog so he does exactly what you tell him and he never dragged me through hedges or anything like that. Besides, Mrs Bamber gave me five pounds a week to walk Gregory and always invited me inside on Saturday for my pay and a glass of Coke. Since I'm planning to be a billionaire like Bill Gates when I grow up I could do with the money. And since my mother won't have fizzy drinks in the house (she says sugar is the enemy of the people) I liked the Coke, too. But most of all I liked being in the Bambers' house, which wasn't anything like our house. It was clean and neat and modern, like the Bambers themselves.

All that ended with my mother's declaration of war, of course. After that, I wasn't allowed near the Bambers, in case they tried to pump me for information about the Keep Our Planet Greeners. My mother said Mr Bamber wasn't to be trusted, but I sort of thought it was *me* she didn't trust. My mother always said I was a stockbroker waiting to happen. She knew that I dreamed of having parents like the Bambers – you know, ones you could take out in public. And she also knew that I secretly agreed with Mr Bamber about chopping down the woods and digging up the fields. Mr Bamber called it progress and so did I. My mother called it rape and murder.

So that was why I was sitting at my bedroom window on the evening the Bambers brought the new kid home for the first time, watching the street for their return.

My father was in his studio making another fountain no one would buy. My mother was in the living-room chairing an emergency meeting of Keep Our Planet Green. The Greeners had collected about a trillion signatures of people who were against chopping down the woods and building houses, but half of them had gone missing from Caroline Ludgate's post van. My mother wanted me to join the meeting, but I told her I had homework to do. Mrs Ludgate was not a very together person, if you asked me. She was always late for meetings because she had to go back for things she'd forgotten so many times. It didn't surprise me that she'd lost the petitions. Besides, the country looked green enough to me.

But mostly, I wanted to see what the new kid looked like.

I knew all about the new kid because everyone in town knew about the new kid. There was an article about Mr and Mrs Bamber in the local paper, with a picture of them holding a blurred photograph that sort of looked like a young boy. And they were even interviewed on the evening news. My mother had been on the news a couple of times – usually when she was blocking a road or screaming at someone – but this was different. Mr and Mrs Bamber were on the news for deciding, out of the goodness of their hearts, to adopt an orphan from South America. It was even more impressive than the time Mr Bamber had dinner with the Prime Minister. I read the article and I watched the interview on TV, so I knew that the new kid was twelve years old, like I am. Which I reckoned was pretty ironic. I wasn't what you could call really popular at school. All my life I'd wanted a best friend, especially one who was normal and lived close by. If I had a best friend close by, I'd have someone to ride my bike to school with, and someone to sit with at lunch, and someone to hang around with in the afternoon. I'd never have to play Monopoly with my computer again. But now that a potentially suitable candidate for the position of my best friend was finally moving in virtually next door, I wasn't allowed to play with him. If that's not ironic, what is? Especially since *I* hadn't declared war on the Bambers. *I* couldn't see anything wrong with the Bambers. I liked their posh house and their big car, and I liked *them*. Not that I really knew them or anything, the way I knew my parents and my grandparents and my aunt and uncle and baby Gertie. But I liked them because they were so perfect and normal and did ordinary things. And they were always calm and pleasant, unlike some people I knew.

To tell the truth, it sometimes seemed to me that some horrible mistake had been made, and that I really belonged with the Bambers more than I belonged with the Blues. For one thing, I look more like the Bambers than the Blues. The Bambers are short and compact, not big and gangling like my family. For another, I wouldn't have minded having parents who wear nice clothes and have important jobs and always behave properly. It would have made a pleasant change.

Leaves scuttled down the road in the rain and wind.

I wiped the window where my breath had

clouded it over and leaned as far out as I could. The rain made it hard to see through my glasses, but I could see well enough to know that there was still no sign of the Bambers' car. I sighed. What was keeping them?

This may sound stupid, but I'd been waiting for the Bambers to bring the new kid home for months. Which just shows you how bored and lonely I must have been. I spent a lot of time imagining the new kid and what the two of us would have done together if I had normal parents and not the ones I had. I could see us playing Monopoly, and messing about with the computer, and riding our bikes while we talked about chess strategies. I even imagined that the new kid would find my jokes funny – which was something no one else did.

I was just picturing the new kid laughing over a joke I'd made when something occurred to me. What if the Bambers were late getting back because something had gone wrong with the adoption? Nothing ever went wrong for the Bambers as far as I could see, so this wasn't anything I'd thought of before.

My glasses always slide off my nose when I frown. I pushed them back and thought of the things that could have gone wrong with the adoption. I couldn't think of any. I mean, it wasn't likely that the new kid had decided that he didn't want to live with the Bambers, was it? If my parents had turned up to collect him, gibbering about endangered species and musical fountains, he might ask for a few seconds to think things over. But no normal child could see Mr and Mrs Bamber in their immaculate suits and gold jewellery and pleasant smiles and say to himself, "Well, I think I'll stay in the orphanage in storm-ravaged South America rather than go with them." I wouldn't have, I can tell you that.

I wiped the rain from my glasses for the billionth time.

On the other hand, I reasoned, the Bambers might have changed *their* minds about the new kid. This made sense.

I stared out at the Bambers' house. My mother said that the Bambers' house was so perfect because they had a woman to do the housework and a man to do the garden, and (ignoring the fact that I'm the only person in the house who ever puts anything away) no children to mess everything up. The last part of my mother's words stuck in my mind. Maybe the new kid was messy. My mother was right, most children were. I didn't know anyone else my age who kept their room as neat and clean as I did. Even my teacher said she'd never heard of a twelve-year-old boy who alphabetized all his books and toys and labelled his drawers. Maybe the Bambers suddenly realized that they didn't want some kid messing up their house after all.

I was so convinced that Mr and Mrs Bamber had left the new kid where he was and gone out for dinner, that I was about to abandon my post at the window when a car turned the corner at the end of the road. Excited, I banged my head as the Bambers' black BMW pulled into their drive. I could just make out Mr Bamber behind the steering wheel, and Mrs Bamber beside him. There was a dark figure in the back seat that couldn't be Gregory because he was much smaller, and anyway I could hear Gregory yapping from inside the house.

I leaned as far out of the window as I could, but from that distance, and with the rain and everything, the Bambers and their house and car were more or less just blurs.

The blur that was Mr Bamber got out first. He had a black raincoat over his suit. I could tell from the way his head was tilted that he had his mobile phone pressed to his ear. Mr Bamber never went anywhere without his mobile phone. Even in the interview on the news his mobile was on the table. It drove my mother mad. "Who on earth does he think is going to ring him in the middle of a television programme?" she'd screamed. I thought it was pretty cool personally. It made him seem really important. Which, of course, he was.

Mr Bamber strode up the path to the front door. Mrs Bamber got out next. She was the blur wearing the light-coloured raincoat and a matching hat. She opened the back door of the car at the same moment that Mr Bamber opened the door to the house. Gregory bounded out into the rain at the same moment that the new kid stepped on to the drive.

The new kid was not what I expected. For one thing, he wasn't small and compact like Mr and Mrs Bamber. The new kid was tall and wide and seemed to have an awful lot of legs and arms. He was wearing a hat. It wasn't a sombrero or anything like that, though. It was an old man's hat.

I squeezed myself through the window for a better look. My room is on the second floor, at the top of the house. I climbed out carefully, holding on to the frame. The roof sloped a lot more than I'd thought.

Gregory was racing down the front path to greet Mrs Bamber. He was going as fast as his tiny legs could carry him, yapping away. Then, about halfway down the path, he stopped so suddenly that he fell over.

I leaned forward to get a better view.

Gregory had stopped yapping, too. He quivered in place for several seconds, his eyes on the new kid. Then, with one shrill howl of horror, he ran back into the house with his tail between his legs.

That's when I fell off the roof. I was wearing my tiger slippers, which aren't actually meant for outdoor wear, and my foot slipped on the wet tiles.

At the exact moment that I started sliding off the roof, the new kid turned and looked up at me. I saw him. I know it sounds weird. You'd think I was too busy breaking my neck to *see* anything, but I did. And then I saw him smile. It was the sort of smile the dentist gives you when they're about to tell you that you don't have any cavities this check-up. Even though I was about to crash to the ground, the new kid's smile made me feel calm.

Then the next weird thing happened.

One second I was sort of hurtling through space, and the next second something wrapped itself around me. It was soft and warm like a fur glove. I drifted to the ground and landed between my mother's favourite rhododendron and my father's dragon fountain. I couldn't believe my luck. If I'd broken either of those things the pair of them would have killed me.

Mrs Bamber missed the whole thing. She shut the car door and started towards the house.

"Come inside," she called. "You don't want to catch a cold."

With a nod in my direction, the new kid turned and followed her into the house.

And I sat there in our front garden, wondering how I could tell that the new kid's eyes were blue.

I HAVE A VISIT

The Keep Our Planet Green meeting was just ending when I got back into the house. The usual Greeners were in a huddle in the living-room. There were a lot of people in the area who belonged to the group, but no more than a handful of them ever showed up for meetings and stuff. There was Mrs Ludgate, the post-woman, and Mr Meadows, a local farmer, but I didn't know any of the others by name. I tried to stay aloof. They were all talking at once, as usual, and didn't notice me dripping in the hallway, even though I looked pretty green because of the grass stains on my shirt and trousers.

I cleared my throat loudly, but they were making so much noise themselves that they didn't hear me.

Now that I'd recovered from the shock of falling off the roof, I was beginning to feel a

18

little shaky. I mean, it really was a miracle that I hadn't hurt myself. Or broken the stupid fountain or my mother's prize bush. I reckoned I was entitled to a little sympathy for what I'd been through.

I slammed the door so hard the wall shook. No one noticed that, either.

My mother started waving her arms in the air and shouting. The cluster of leaves that was caught in her hair shook. Unlike Mrs Bamber, my mother was never neat and presentable, not even when she tried. Tonight, however, she had sunk below even her own low standards. Besides having leaves in her hair, my mother's old jeans and faded shirt were covered with dirt, and her face was smeared with ink. Most of the time my mother looks like she wrestles hogs for a living, but on days when Keep Our Planet Green meets she looks like she wrestles hogs with leaky ballpoint pens grasped in their trotters.

"This isn't the end," announced my mother. "I admit losing all those petitions is a bit of a setback, but with a little extra work we can replace them in no time."

"You're right about 'no time'," said one of the Greeners. "'No time' is precisely what we have. The Council votes next week. They're not going to postpone the meeting again."

My mother had had to beg for a little more time after Mrs Ludgate lost the petitions.

19

Fortunately for the Greeners, one of the councillors had the flu and another was in Bali, so she was able to get an extra week.

I cleared my throat and stamped my feet. And was still ignored. You had to be a tree or a bird or something like that to get any attention from that lot.

"Well, it looks like the end to me," agreed Caroline Ludgate. "I feel awful about losing those petitions, but we have to face the facts. There isn't time to replace them, and without them we don't have nearly enough signatures to make the Council listen to us."

Alf Meadows, the farmer, nodded. "You know I hate to give up, Grace," he said to my mother, "but I'm afraid I have to agree with Caroline. Bamber's won. Maybe not fairly and squarely, but he has won. We might as well save our strength for the next fight."

Silence followed this remark. Everyone looked from Alf Meadows to my mother.

I took advantage of the sudden quiet to cry "Mum!" I made my voice sort of shrill, so she'd know something bad had happened.

My mother didn't hear me.

"*Et tu*, Alf?" she cried dramatically, her eyes on Mr Meadows. "Are you going to desert us now, when we need you most?"

I called, "Mum!" a little louder this time.

Alf Meadows said, "With all due respect, Grace, you don't need me, or anyone else, now. The time has come for you to admit the truth. It's over. Bamber gets his houses and his golf course and makes a lot of money, and we lose our woods, and probably get a new road we don't want to boot. There's nothing more we can do."

I moved closer to the Greeners and gave myself a shake.

"Mum!" I cried in a small, terrified voice guaranteed to move the hardest heart. "Mum!"

It was the shake that did it. A fine spray of water settled over several of the Greeners, including their chairperson, my female parent, Grace Blue.

"Oh, for heaven's sake, Elmo!" A leaf fluttered from my mother's hair as she turned to scowl at me. "What is it now?"

Personally, I thought her attitude was a little unfair. I never interrupted my mother during her Green meetings like other children would. In fact, I always went out of my way to be as far away from them as possible. I didn't see why she had to carry on like I was always bothering her.

"I fell off the roof," I said simply.

Told that her child had fallen off the roof, a normal mother would demonstrate shock, horror and maternal concern at the news. She would gasp and tears would fill her eyes. My mother just looked suspicious.

"What on earth were you doing on the roof?" she demanded.

The question was so unexpected that I answered truthfully. "I was trying to see the new kid," I explained. "In the car. And then—"

My mother frowned and another leaf drifted to the floor.

"You were spying on the Bambers?"

I backtracked quickly.

"I wasn't spying. I was looking. I just wanted to see what the new kid's like."

"It doesn't matter what he's like now," said my mother. "The Bambers will turn him into a greedy green-killer like themselves in no time at all."

"Greedy green-killer" was among the more polite names my mother called Mr Bamber. Since Mrs Bamber was married to Mr Bamber, she was a "greedy green-killer" too.

"You know what I think about spying," my mother went on.

I did know what she thought about spying. Not a lot. A friend of Mr Bamber's joined the Greeners the spring before, pretending to be interested in saving what remained of the countryside, but really to spy on the group for Mr Bamber. My mother caught him taping a meeting. My mother didn't approve.

"But, Mum—" I was determined to get the conversation away from spying and back to me. "Mum, you're not paying attention. *I fell off the roof!* Don't you understand? I might have been killed."

"That's what happens to spies," said my mother.

I gazed at her in horror. She really was incredible. If I'd been a badger cub or something she'd have burst into tears at the thought of me falling off a roof.

It was Caroline Ludgate who finally showed some concern for me.

"Did you really fall off the roof, Elmo?" she asked. "Are you all right?"

"Yes, I really fell off the roof," I answered. "And, yes, I'm fine."

Mrs Ludgate peered down at me, looking for cuts and bruises.

"There's not a scratch on you!" she said in amazement. "Are you sure you haven't broken any bones?"

A few of the other Greeners started making sympathetic sounds, too.

At last I had an audience.

"That was the strange thing," I told Mrs Ludgate. "I didn't really fall to the ground, I just sort of floated down." I pointed to the latest leaf to leave my mother's head. "Like that."

Mrs Ludgate smiled in that way adults smile when they're not really listening to what a child is saying.

"That's nice," she murmured. "You're a very lucky little boy."

My mother's mind was already back on Mr Bamber and the lost petitions.

"If only we were as lucky..." she mused.

"We don't need luck," said Alf Meadows. "What we need is a miracle."

Everybody started talking at once again.

"I'm going to my room to change out of these wet clothes before I catch pneumonia," I shouted over the uproar.

Nobody even glanced at me as I stomped out of the room.

I was pretty upset, I can tell you that.

"Stupid woods," I muttered as I climbed the stairs to my room. "I hope Mr Bamber cuts them all down."

I was so upset that I shut my door behind me and threw myself on my bed without even worrying about wrinkling the bedspread or getting it wet or anything. I didn't even take my slippers off first.

I was so upset that I didn't realize I wasn't alone until I heard the beep of my computer.

THE NEW KID ISN'T WHAT I EXPECTED

Sitting at my computer table in the far corner of the room was the new kid. He had his back to me as he tapped the keyboard. He wasn't wearing his hat now, and I could see that his hair wasn't short, like all the other boys at school wore theirs, but tied back in a small ponytail. The monitor cast a pale blue light over his head. I'd never noticed that it did that before, but I'd never seen anybody else sitting at my computer before, either.

"Oi!" I said. "What do you think you're doing?"

He didn't turn round. He was even bigger in my room than he was in the Bambers' drive-way. I reckoned he had to be at least a head taller than I was, and most of it was legs.

Taptaptap. Beepbeepbeep.

"I was waiting for you."

Taptaptap. Beepbeepbeep.

"Waiting for me?" I was too surprised to say anything else.

The new kid shrugged.

"The Bambers are about as interesting as watching cement set. I couldn't stand more than a few minutes of them. All he talks about is money and all she does is agree with him."

I didn't believe him. How could people who drove a BMW and a Porsche be uninteresting? I got to my feet. Standing, I was as tall as the new kid was sitting down.

"But how did you get in here?" I walked over and stood behind him. "You didn't come through the front door. I would've seen you."

The new kid turned round and smiled. "I came through the window."

I barely heard "I came through the window". I was too shocked over something else. My mother's very into "our multi-racial society", but the Bambers' adopted son was a multi-racial society of one. His hair was black, his skin was brown, his eyes were shaped like almonds, but were blue. Not that that was what was so shocking.

"You're a girl!" I didn't even pretend to hide my surprise. "I thought you were a boy."

The new kid went back to her game. "Clerical mix-up. It happens all the time."

"But—but—" I stammered. I'd been sure the new kid was a boy. I'd read the article in the paper; I'd watched Mr and Mrs Bamber on

TV. Mr Bamber said he'd always wanted a son. He'd said the new kid was twelve years old.

It was as if she could read my mind. "I *am* twelve years old," she informed me rather sharply, "and my name's Kuba." For an orphan from South America she had a weird accent. She sounded American to me. "And that's because I learned my English from American aid workers."

I ignored the fact that she really did seem able to read my mind.

"But me and my mum *saw* Mrs Bamber in the boys' department a couple of weeks ago. Shopping for *you*."

"She should have waited," said my new neighbour. "I told you, there was a clerical mix-up. Someone typed in *male* where they should have typed in *female*."

I couldn't believe it. This was not the best friend I'd been waiting for my whole life. No way. I'd been expecting a small, neat boy rather like myself, possibly with glasses, definitely with a pleasant and polite manner. I hadn't been expecting a giant girl who broke into people's houses.

"How did you say you got in here?"

She nodded across the room. "The window."

I looked over at the window.

"Don't be ridiculous. You couldn't come in the window. It's impossible. It's two floors up." And I should know, I'd gone out that way not that long ago.

"Nothing is impossible," said Kuba. "Not if you know how." She turned to me with another smile. "Now sit down. We need to talk."

I get pushed around sometimes by other boys because I'm small and I don't like the same things they like (which are mainly football and horror films), but I wasn't going to be pushed around in my own room. And definitely not by a *girl*. Not even by one who's bigger than I am.

"We don't have anything to talk about," I snapped. "Since you're so good at climbing through windows, you can go out the same way you say you came in."

But Kuba wasn't a girl who was easily bullied. Probably because she was built like a tower block. She pointed to the monitor. She wasn't playing a game at all. At least she wasn't playing any game that I owned. There on the computer screen were Mr and Mrs Bamber. They were in their kitchen. Mrs Bamber was taking something out of the refrigerator. Mr Bamber was opening a bottle of wine while he talked on his mobile.

"There isn't much time," said Kuba. "They'll be calling me down to dinner in ten minutes. I have to get back or they'll know I was gone."

It's amazing how quickly you can get used to being shocked.

"What are the Bambers doing on my computer?" I demanded. It really was too much! And then, realizing how confused I was, I asked again, "How did you get in here?"

Kuba got up from my chair and went over and sat on the bed. Her arms were still folded in front of her and the blue light of the computer still shone on the top of her head.

"I should think you'd want to thank me for saving your life," she said sourly. "Instead of asking me stupid questions."

I made a disbelieving face.

"Oh, right ... *you* saved my life."

She raised her eyebrows. The light hovering around the top of her head shimmered.

"Well, what else do you think stopped you from falling? Your parachute?"

Since I had no idea what had stopped me from falling I didn't say anything. I just glared back at her.

"Besides," Kuba continued. "I couldn't let you damage that beautiful fountain. I haven't seen anything that exquisite since the Renaissance."

I wasn't exactly sure what the Renaissance was, but I knew you had to be over twelve to remember it. I continued to glare.

"You know," Kuba continued, "you'd save us both a lot of time if you asked me *why* I'm here, rather than how."

"OK," I said, trying to look at her and Mr and Mrs Bamber at the same time. "*Why* are you here?"

I don't know what I thought she was going to say – something like "because I wanted to meet you" would have been all right – but I wasn't really prepared for what she did say.

"Because I'm an undercover angel and I need to talk to you."

I didn't say or do anything for a few seconds. Kuba's words sort of jogged around in my head: "because I'm an undercover angel … because I'm an undercover angel". Then I started to laugh.

"Oh, right!" I spluttered. "Sure you are. An undercover angel from South America come to save the world."

"Not the *whole* world," said Kuba. "Just a tiny part of it."

I spluttered some more. "Where are your wings?"

"Wings are for birds."

I couldn't stop laughing. "You don't look like an angel. You look like a basketball player."

Kuba gave me a very unangelic look.

"And you don't look totally unintelligent, but I could be wrong." She leaned towards me slightly. "Tell me this, Elmo Blue. If I'm not an angel, how did I get into your room? If I'm not an angel, what are the Bambers doing on your monitor? If I'm not an angel, why didn't you hurt yourself when you fell off the roof?"

The best thing to do when someone asks you a question – or a few questions – that you can't answer is ignore them.

"I don't know," I snapped. "And I don't care. I don't even care why your hair's all blue. I just want you to go home and leave me alone."

Kuba shook her head. "Not everyone can see it, you know." She flashed her dentist-giving-you-good-news smile. "It's my halo."

That did it. I grabbed hold of her hand and pulled her to her feet.

"What do you think I am – stupid?" I screamed. "Only someone who was really stupid would believe that you're an angel. What are you supposed to be doing? Guarding the Bambers?"

Somehow, without me actually noticing, Kuba had got out of my hold and was sitting at the computer again.

"Not the Bambers." She laughed, but not musically, the way you'd think an angel would laugh. Kuba laughed like a giraffe. "The Bambers don't need my help right now." She tapped a couple of keys. "At the moment, I'm here to help your mother."

"My *mother*?" She really did think I was stupid. "You're an angel, and you came all the way to Campton to help my mother? To help her do what?" I went on, my voice thick with sarcasm. "Garden?"

"No." She hit another key. My mother appeared on the computer screen. She was in her "office", the room that used to be the pantry at the back of the kitchen. She had her head on the stack of petitions that weren't lost by Mrs Ludgate and she was crying. I'd never seen my mother cry before. "I'm here to help her stop Mr Bamber."

"Turn that off," I ordered. Crying was a private thing. I didn't want to watch.

Much to my amazement, Kuba hit the keys again. The Bambers' voices filled my room.

I didn't want to, but I couldn't help myself. I gawped at the screen.

Mr Bamber had finished his phone call. He was handing Mrs Bamber her glass. He raised his own glass and touched it to hers.

"Here's to us," said Mr Bamber. "By this time next week we'll be on our way to being millionaires."

"Yes, indeed," said Mrs Bamber. She touched Mr Bamber's glass with hers. "Here's to Kuba. Our own child at last." I'd never seen Mrs Bamber look so happy. "Isn't she wonderful, David? Aren't you thrilled?"

Mr Bamber, however, wasn't thinking about Kuba. He laughed.

"That crazy vegetarian do-gooder across

the street doesn't stand a chance," said Mr Bamber. "Bleeding-heart pain-in-the-bum" and "green ghoul" obviously weren't the only things he called my mother.

"I thought it might be a sign that she turned out to be a girl," Mrs Bamber was saying in her quiet, apologetic way. "I thought you might forget about the Greeners and Grace..."

But Mr Bamber was still having his own conversation. "No, she doesn't stand a chance." He grinned. "Not with half of her precious petitions missing." He touched Mrs Bamber's glass with his again. "The permission is as good as ours."

I was shocked. I admit it. It almost sounded like Mr Bamber was saying that *he'd* stolen the petitions to make sure my mother would lose. But that couldn't be true. Mr Bamber was an important businessman. Important businessmen didn't do things like that.

Kuba was looking at me with a quizzical expression on her face. "Well?"

"It's a trick," I said. It had to be a trick. "Mr Bamber wouldn't cheat like that. He's had dinner with a prime minister."

"So did Hitler," answered Kuba. "And what about that spy last spring?"

I tried not to let on that I was surprised she knew about the spy. I decided to change tack.

"If you're an undercover angel, why are you telling *me*?" I demanded. "Aren't you supposed to keep it a secret? Isn't that what 'undercover' means?"

Kuba made a face that suggested telling me wasn't her idea, or even an idea she thought a particularly good one.

"I have to tell you," she said flatly. "I'm not really meant to directly interfere in people's lives. Not *too* directly. I need *your* help."

"Well you're not going to get it." I was sure of that much. "I just want you to leave me alone."

Kuba stood up as the timer went off on Mrs Bamber's microwave.

"All right," she said sweetly. "I'll leave you alone for now. I've got to go anyway. They'll be calling me to dinner in a minute." She made a face. "Hamburgers."

"What's wrong with that?" Hamburgers didn't seem so awful to me. All the kids I knew loved hamburgers, and I was pretty sure that if I'd ever been allowed to have hamburgers, I'd love them, too.

"Death on a bun," said Kuba. She shuddered. "I'd rather eat soil. But Mr Bamber doesn't believe that anyone under eighteen should be a vegetarian."

"You're a vegetarian?" This surprised me as much as her claim to be an angel. In my school there was only one vegetarian, and I was it. "A vegetarian from South America?"

She rolled her eyes. "Don't you get it? I'm

an angel, not an orphan. I don't come from South America any more than you do."

"Yeah, right…" I said. And then, to get off the subject of angels, I said, "I suppose the Bambers have forbidden you to speak to me."

Kuba shook her head. "Not at all. They *want* me to be friends with you."

I couldn't help feeling a bit chuffed about that. Even though the Bambers thought my mother was a crazy vegetarian, they thought I was the kind of boy they wanted as a friend for their adopted child.

"They do?"

"Uh huh. Mrs Bamber just wants me to make friends and be happy, but Mr Bamber wants me to spy on your mother. He was very disappointed that I wasn't a boy, so you and I could be best mates." She smiled, but there was nothing angelic about it. "Poor Mr Bamber," crooned Kuba. "You should've seen how upset he was when he saw me! He nearly dropped his mobile. He would've sent me back if Mrs Bamber hadn't stopped him."

Now I was really shocked. Not about Mr Bamber wanting a boy, though. About the spying.

"Mr Bamber said that? He told you he wanted you to spy for him?"

"Well, not *me* exactly. He told Mrs Bamber." She winked again. "They don't think I speak much English."

I don't know what, but I was going to say something, only Kuba had gone. I looked at the space where she'd been, and then I looked at the computer. It was off.

I lay down on my bed to wait to be called for supper myself.

Maybe falling off the roof had hurt me more than I'd thought. I was definitely feeling confused.

There was no way I believed that the new kid was an angel. I mean, really – pull the other one. I'm a very logical and scientific sort of person. Everyone else in my family believes in instinct and feelings, but I trust reason. Even if Kuba had had wings I wouldn't have believed her.

But this position did leave a few unanswered questions.

Like why I *didn't* plummet to the ground. And how she got into my room. And, even more puzzling, how my mother and the Bambers got on my computer.

The human ability to reason is an incredible thing. By the time my father called me down to supper I had logical explanations for all of my questions. Every one.

The first explanation was that I didn't crash into the garden because it was a windy night and the baggy shirt I was wearing – my mother always bought everything too large for me –

acted like a parachute.

The second, third and fourth answers were all the same: Kuba was never in my room at all. She didn't talk to me, she didn't give me her opinion on hamburgers, she didn't show me the Bambers and my mother on my monitor. It was a hallucination, like when you're dying of thirst in the desert and you're sure you see a blue pool of water just metres away. The shock from the fall made me *think* that Kuba did all that stuff. But she didn't. I'd imagined the whole thing. What a relief.

Just as I'd expected, my mother didn't look as though she'd been sobbing her heart out less than an hour ago. She was her usual self, sniffing the salad for signs of pesticides and slopping cashew casserole on to everyone's plate. There were still leaves in her hair, and she was still banging on about Mr Bamber and how she was going to stop him from building his houses, even though the other Greeners had given up.

The rest of my family was sympathetic.

"Of course you will, Grace," Grandma and Grandpa kept saying. "Of course you will."

Uncle Cal and Aunt Lucille kept saying, "Of course you will, Grace," too.

My father eats with one hand and doodles designs for fountains on his napkin with the other, but even he kept nodding and saying, "Of course you will, Grace."

The only ones who didn't say anything were baby Gertie and me. Baby Gertie couldn't actually talk yet.

And then my mother said, "So when can you help me get more signatures? Tonight? Tomorrow?"

Grandpa shook his head sadly, his eyes on his plate. "I'm afraid you're going to have to count your mother and me out of this," he said. "We've got the competitions coming up. We can't spare any time." My grandparents have their own dance school over the garage.

My mother bristled. "Not even one afternoon?"

My grandmother shrugged. "There's so much to do, dear..."

My mother turned on Uncle Cal and Aunt Lucille. "What about you two?"

Uncle Cal glanced at Aunt Lucille. Aunt Lucille sighed.

"I'm afraid it's impossible this week, Grace," Aunt Lucille murmured. "We have to get that mural done. We're already over schedule." My Uncle Cal and Aunt Lucille are artists, only they don't paint on canvas, they paint on walls. "Next week we'd be happy to help."

"But next week's too late," shrieked my mother. "You know that. I have to have ten thousand signatures by Thursday. That's the day the Council meets."

"You know I'd love to help you, dear," said my father, "but I really have to finish this fountain I've been working on. It feels urgent."

Only in my family could a fountain feel anything.

My mother's fork clattered on to the table. "Fuller Blue! What are you talking about 'urgent'? You don't think the state of the environment is urgent, too?"

You thought Elmo was about as bad as it could get, didn't you? Fuller is my father's name. Grandpa's name is Monrose. I come from a long line of bad names, handed down from generation to generation like a gene for big ears. It's our family tradition.

"But it's about to come together," moaned my father. "The whole design. It's revolutionary. If I stop now it may take me months to get back to where I am now."

My mother leaned back in her chair and glared at the rest of us.

"What about you, Gertie?" she asked acidly. "Would you like to help me collect signatures?"

Gertie – who did little more than cry, sleep, wet her nappies, cry and throw up – was screaming and waving a fistful of mashed potatoes in the air.

"I'll help."

I only realized it was me who'd spoken when everyone else turned to look at me.

"*You?*" My mother looked as shocked as I'd felt when I thought I saw Kuba sitting at my computer. "You told me collecting signatures was beneath you."

I couldn't seem to keep my mouth shut.

"No, I didn't. I said it was embarrassing." My mouth smiled. "But I've got over that."

She frowned. She couldn't have looked more worried if I'd been a sparrow-hawk with a broken foot. "Maybe we'd better take you to casualty," said my mother. "You must have fallen on your head."

MY FIRST DAY AS AN ENVIRONMENTAL ACTIVIST

When I woke up the next morning and saw the rain pouring down, I wondered if maybe I *had* fallen on my head.

I mean, what normal child volunteers to spend his Sunday squelching through a storm, begging people to sign a petition when he could be dry and warm at home? Even a child who was in danger of being roped into a tango lesson by someone who didn't have a partner wouldn't be that stupid. What was I thinking of, offering to help my mother with her petitions on a Sunday? Especially since I *did* think it was embarrassing. I wasn't that happy to be seen with my mother at the best of times, but when she was in Greener mode was the worst.

I got out of bed slowly, trying to remember just what it was that had made me shout out "I'll help" like that. It was as if someone had taken over my voice. I put on my warmest socks and two shirts.

It took a long time to get to the town centre, because my mother doesn't drive an ordinary car. Of course. Polluting the atmosphere with toxic fumes is against her principles. She has a bike with a trailer at the back that she uses for work and for shopping and stuff like that. But when she has to haul something big, like a couple of trees or a ton of manure, she uses the milk float. It doesn't say *Dansworth's Dairy* on the front like it used to – she painted it green with *Grace Blue, Gardener* in yellow – but it's still a milk float. She decided to take the milk float because of the weather. For some reason she seemed to think the milk float would provide more protection from the rain than a bicycle. She was wrong. Not only could we have got there faster if we'd biked, but we'd have been a lot drier when we arrived, too.

All the way, my mother banged on about how important this was, and how she knew that we'd get enough signatures if we really tried, and how happy she was that I was finally taking an interest in the environment.

I said "Yeah" and "Um" and stuff like that, and huddled in my raincoat. I could only pray that none of the kids from school who pushed me around saw me. I'd never live it down if they found out my mother drove a milk float.

My mother stood on one end of the street, in front of McDonald's, and I stood at the

42

other, in front of Gap. My mother is against plastic bags, but she can bend her principles when it's really necessary, so we each had a clipboard with a sheaf of papers in a carrier bag so they wouldn't get wet.

There weren't many people out. Most people were at home doing what my mother calls the "dead animal ritual", which means having Sunday lunch. After lunch, they'd curl up on the sofa and watch TV. There was usually a good film on Sunday afternoon. My canvas trainers leaked (no leather allowed in our house), and water trickled down the back of my neck. I wanted to be at home watching a film, too.

In the first two hours I got three signatures. It was really discouraging. I couldn't understand how my mother could put herself through this day after day, year after year. Maybe Mr Bamber was right, and my mother really was mad.

I'd thought that all I'd have to do was say "Excuse me, but would you like to sign this petition?" very politely and that would be it. But it wasn't. Everybody had an excuse. If they were going *into* a shop, they told me they'd sign on the way out. If they were coming *out*, they told me they had to get to their car before the traffic warden did. A lot of people raced right past me without even looking at me, never mind saying anything. It was easy enough for them to do. They'd see me ahead of them, lower their umbrellas and charge by.

The first two signatures I got were from old ladies who felt sorry for me. One of them even offered to give me money so I could get a nice cup of tea and some fries in McDonald's. I would have loved a nice cup of tea right then, I can tell you. But my mother doesn't like McDonald's either. I'd missed every birthday party I was ever invited to because they were all held at McDonald's and my mother wouldn't let me go. Which explains why I had no friends. My mother was planted right in front of the golden arches, so there was no way I could sneak in for a quick snack without her seeing me. A single chip could destroy all the pride she had in me for finally caring about the environment.

The third signature I got was from a woman from Australia.

I finished explaining about the valuable, ancient woods and the fields full of wild-flowers, and the beautiful, historically inter-esting old cemetery, and the lovely lake where children used to boat and swim, and she said, "I'm sorry, honey, I'm just visiting."

This made sense to me. I mean, they weren't *her* trees, were they? I was about to say I under-stood when a voice behind me cut me off.

"Just visiting the planet?" asked the voice.

Both the woman from Australia and I

44

looked round.

I admit it. I was a little surprised to see Kuba standing there in her wrinkled jacket and her old hat, totally dry and smiling her everything's-wonderful smile. In order to be behind me like that, she had to have come out of Gap. But she couldn't have come out of Gap, because I'd been standing there for nearly two hours and she hadn't gone in. But this time I knew she wasn't a hallucination caused by my fall from the house because the woman from Australia said, "What?"

I gave Kuba a nudge and muttered, "Go away."

Kuba ignored me completely.

"Are you just visiting the planet?" she asked sweetly. "Because if you are, then I can see that you wouldn't be very interested in what happens around here."

"What are you doing?" I hissed. And then, forgetting that she hadn't really been in my room the night before, I added, "I thought you weren't meant to interfere."

"Within reason," Kuba hissed back. Her smile was like sunshine, and shining on the woman from Australia. "What galaxy is it you come from?" she asked politely.

"Australia." The woman from Australia closed her umbrella. It had suddenly stopped raining.

Down the street I could see my mother

looking in my direction. I waved.

"Now that's different," Kuba was saying. "Australia *is* on this planet. Which means that anything that affects us here eventually affects you there."

Drawn by the unexpected appearance of the sun, more people appeared on the street.

Kuba said to me, "Isn't it true that everything on our planet is interconnected, Elmo?"

A couple of people had stopped and were standing beside the woman from Australia. All of them looked at me.

I tried hard to ignore my mother and her causes. But my twelve years of living with Grace Blue, champion of the endangered species of this world, were obviously stronger than my desire not to hear a word she said. More or less on automatic, I started to explain all the stuff I knew because my mother never stopped talking about it. I explained about trees and the atmosphere, and pollution and the atmosphere, and all about the hole in the ozone layer and the sinking ionosphere, and how everybody's weather was changing and whole species were dying – including humans – and how more would die if we didn't do something about it. Ironically enough, scientific fact actually backed my mother's beliefs.

By the end of my speech, several people were queuing up to sign my petition. I'd just handed the clipboard over to the woman from

Australia when I spotted Mr Bamber at the back of the crowd. I glanced over my shoulder, but Kuba was gone.

Mr Bamber was staring at me so hard that I thought he was going to say something to me. You know, something like "Hello" or "What are you doing here, Elmo?" But he didn't.

In his usual clear, pleasant and reasonable voice Mr Bamber said, "What sort of world do we live in when a group of adults will stand around listening to a child give a physics lecture?" He said it loudly.

Even more loudly, the woman from Australia said, "'And a little child shall lead them...'"

I knew that was a quote from the Bible because of my grandmother. My grandmother loves the Old Testament.

Mr Bamber laughed. "Where's this little child going to lead you?" he chuckled. "To the sweet shop?"

Not *this* little child. Not with *my* mother, he wouldn't.

WEIRDER AND WEIRDER

My mother was over the moon.

"Can you believe it?" she shrieked above the whirr of the milk float as we drove home. "I can't believe it! A thousand signatures. A thousand signatures in one afternoon! If you don't call that a miracle, what do you call it?"

I didn't have an answer for that. Well, I *had* an answer, but it wasn't the one I wanted.

"It's really good," I said.

My mother was staring through the windscreen, grinning at the road ahead.

"It's a miracle," she repeated. "I really feel that God is on our side on this one." She turned her grin on me. "Don't you, Elmo?"

This was another point I didn't feel I could argue. The fact that everybody else saw Kuba this time sort of destroyed my theory that she was just a hallucination. I was reading Sherlock Holmes at the time. Holmes says that

48

once you eliminate the impossible, whatever's left, no matter how improbable, is the truth. Which meant that Kuba probably was an angel.

"I don't know where they all came from." My mother sighed. "All those people..."

I knew exactly where they'd come from. I'd seen my mother stand in front of McDonald's for two whole days and be happy if she got a hundred signatures. To get a thousand signatures on a Sunday afternoon in Campton High Street was right up there with Jesus feeding hundreds of people with a couple of fish and loaves of bread if you asked me. The only explanation was that Kuba had brought them.

"I reckon it was the sunshine," I muttered. It was something to say. Something better than, "Well, you do realize Kuba Bamber's an angel, don't you?"

"Um..." said my mother. "The sunshine... That was another miracle, wasn't it?"

The thing was, I didn't see what Kuba being an angel really had to do with *me*. It was my mother she was meant to be helping, so why couldn't she leave me alone?

This was one of the things I wanted to think about on the long ride home. Mr Bamber was the other. He'd been my role model ever since the Bambers moved in across the road, only now I was beginning to wonder if I was wrong about him. He'd been his usual smiling self today, but he wasn't very nice. "Smile, and smile, and be a villain", as my grandmother liked to say.

My mother, however, wouldn't let me think about anything. She couldn't stop talking.

"If we can do this every day between now and Thursday, Mr Bamber won't be playing golf in Campton in this lifetime," said my mother. She gave me a big smile. "And you, Elmo! You were brilliant. You're a natural activist. The way you drew the crowds..."

The last thing I needed was for my mother to think I had a talent for getting people to sign petitions. She'd have me standing on street corners for the rest of my life.

"It wasn't just *me,*" I said modestly.

My mother nodded. "Oh, you mean that girl."

I didn't mean that girl at all. I'd been hoping she hadn't noticed Kuba. What I meant was that I thought public opinion was on the Greeners' side for a change.

I stared back at her blankly. "Girl?"

My mother laughed. "Yes, the girl in the hat. The one who was standing with you. Who is she?"

I was going to deny all knowledge. She wasn't standing *with* me, I was going to say. She was just standing *near* me. But then it occurred to me that telling my mother who Kuba was (within reason) was probably the

50

fastest and easiest way of making Kuba disappear that I was going to find. My mother didn't want me anywhere near the Bambers. She didn't want me fraternizing with the enemy. She would put her foot down, and she'd make sure that Kuba Bamber never bothered me again.

"She's the new kid," I told her. "You know, the one the Bambers adopted."

"Ah… So that explains what Old Building Breath was doing there. I thought he was just lurking." She frowned thoughtfully. "I thought they'd adopted a boy," said my mother. "Isn't that what it said in the paper?"

I explained about the clerical error. "You know, someone typed *male* when they were meant to type *female*."

"Bureaucracies," muttered my mother. Her face clouded over for a second. She likes bureaucracies about as much as she likes McDonald's. But she cheered up again straight away. "So, how did you happen to meet her?"

I've always thought of myself as a pretty honest person, but Grace Blue never fails to make me feel shifty.

"Meet who?"

I could hardly hear her sigh because it sounded a lot like the noise of the milk float.

"Who are we talking about, Elmo? David Attenborough? The Bambers' new daughter, of course."

I swallowed a small stone that had suddenly materialized in my throat.

"She just came up to me." I hoped my mother could hear the surprise and shock in my voice. "I know I'm not meant to talk to her, Mum, but I couldn't stop her. Really."

Demonstrating the lack of logic for which she is famous, my mother said, "But why should you want to stop her? Why shouldn't you talk to her?"

I couldn't believe that she was asking *me* that question. Not after the way she carried on last spring. Last spring Grace Blue not only stormed through the house calling Mr Bamber every name she could think of, but she threatened to board up the front window so she wouldn't have to see the Bambers even accidentally. My father only stopped her because it would have destroyed our view of the dragon fountain as well.

"Because of Mr Bamber," I reminded her. "Because he wants to build the development."

"But that has nothing to do with—" She took her eyes off the road to give me a questioning look.

"Kuba," I filled in for her.

"It has nothing to do with Kuba," said my mother. "She's just a child."

I wouldn't be so sure about that, I thought.

This time she not only took her eyes off the road, she took her hands off the wheel. It was probably just as well that we were only doing five miles an hour.

"Oh, Elmo!" cried my mother. She frowned at me as though she was wondering what I used instead of a brain. "Did you think you weren't allowed to make friends with Kuba? Is that what you thought?"

At the moment, it was what I was praying for.

"Well..."

"I just don't want you hanging round the Bambers," explained my mother. "I wouldn't put it past Old Building Breath to try and worm information about the Greeners out of you. But as for Kuba" – she didn't quite laugh – "I should think the poor girl's already bored out of her brain over there. All Build-it-high Bamber ever does is yammer on the phone, and all poor Arabella does is whatever he says. It must be about as much fun as scrubbing the floor with a toothbrush."

Or standing in the rain for hours with a carrier bag full of petitions.

"She seems fine to me."

I don't think my mother heard me.

"I want you to tell Kuba that she's welcome in our house at any time," she was saying. "Any time, morning, noon or night. You understand that, Elmo? We all want to make her feel at home. Even Gertie."

Then maybe they should start teaching

Gertie how to play a harp.

I tried to look relieved. "Thanks," I mumbled. "That's great."

I couldn't wait to tell Kuba.

It was my grandfather's turn to cook that night. It is true that I don't like seaweed as much as he does (nobody who isn't a fish likes seaweed as much as my grandfather), but that wasn't why I decided that I couldn't face a meal with my family. I was too wound up about Kuba. If I didn't do something soon, my mother was bound to bump into her one day and invite her to dinner. Then I'd never get rid of her.

I told my mother I was exhausted from our triumphant afternoon.

"I just want to curl up in bed," I said. I held up the library's copy of *The Complete Sherlock Holmes*. "And read."

My mother patted my shoulder. "Of course. You must be wiped out. All that talking..." She patted my head. "I want you to know that I'm very proud of you, Elmo. You really were brilliant today."

When I won the Junior Computer Whiz competition all Grace Blue said was, "Well, isn't that nice?" I wasn't used to being praised. It made me nervous.

"So it's all right if I go to my room?"

"Of course." She smiled. She patted my

shoulder again. "Just wait one minute, I'm not letting you go to bed hungry."

Lucky me.

Carrying a bowl of seaweed soup, a hunk of seaweed bread spread with something and seaweed, and Sherlock Holmes, I cautiously approached my room on tiptoe.

I couldn't see any light coming from under the door, but I put my ear against it to make sure. There was nothing inside making any sound. The coast was clear.

Once I was safely inside, I put on the bedside light and made myself comfortable. I didn't bother with my supper, I knew what to expect. The Greeners once took me with them to picket the sea and I fell in. That's what Monrose Blue's soup and bread tasted like: the polluted North Sea.

I found the page I was on and started to read. I thought it would help me to relax.

I really was exhausted, though, because pretty soon the words were sort of swimming together. I rubbed my eyes and wiped my glasses and started again. Not only were the words all melting, but the black and white print had turned into blobs of colour.

Because of my scientific nature, I was really interested in this. I'd never experienced an optical illusion before. I forgot about being exhausted and sat very still, waiting to see what would happen next.

Something started to whine. I'd never heard of an optical illusion with sound. I glanced over in case my computer had suddenly turned itself on, but the screen was dark.

I looked back at the open pages of Sherlock Holmes.

The colours were forming patterns. And then the patterns made images.

I was staring down at *A Study in Scarlet*, but I was seeing the Bambers' dining-room.

Mr and Mrs Bamber and Kuba were sitting around the enormous table. The Bambers' table was wooden, but it shone so much that it almost looked like it was made of dark brown glass. When I used to go into the Bambers' house on a Saturday, there was always a vase of flowers on the dining-room table (as opposed to the bits of fountain and Greeners' leaflets that were always on ours), but now there were candles instead. And not only did all the dishes match, they even had little plates for their bread. In our house you were lucky to get a plate for your meal, never mind a separate one for the bread.

The Kuba sitting in the Bambers' dining-room was not the Kuba who'd been in my room the night before or the one who described the ecosystem to the woman from Australia. The Kuba in the dining-room was wearing a dress and had shiny clips in her hair. She smiled sweetly and spoke softly. She seemed almost *demure*. Demure was not a word I'd ever used before (who did, except for my grandmother?), but it was the only one I could think of that fitted.

Kuba was pushing bits of food around on her plate and Mrs Bamber was watching her and asking her questions. "Do you like the meat, Kuba?", "Have you had potatoes like that before?", "Would you like a little more gravy?" After each question, Kuba smiled and answered in stiff, flat words, as if she'd learned her English from a computer program. Mr Bamber was talking on his mobile. Gregory was squashed under Mrs Bamber's chair with his eyes shut. It was Gregory who was whining. Rather pitifully, if you ask me.

"I'll ring you back!" shouted Mr Bamber. He slammed his phone down next to his plate and turned to Mrs Bamber accusingly. "What in heaven's name is wrong with that dog?" he demanded. "He hasn't shut up since we sat down. I can barely hear myself think."

Mrs Bamber stopped smiling at Kuba and got really involved in cutting up her meat.

"I really don't know," she said pleasantly. "Although I do believe it is a full moon tonight."

Funnily enough, Grace Blue would have understood exactly what she meant. My mother has a lot of time for the moon. But Mr Bamber didn't.

"Full moon?" He glared at Mrs Bamber as though she'd informed him it was raining in Buenos Aires. "What does the moon have to do with it?"

Mrs Bamber started cutting her carrots into tiny bits.

"I'm sure I read that dogs are affected by the phases of the moon," she mumbled. "Unlike the stock market."

Mr Bamber missed the crack about the stock market.

"Well that dog's going to be affected by being put outdoors if he doesn't stop carrying on like that," said Mr Bamber. "How am I supposed to conduct my business with him wailing like that?"

Without raising her head from her plate, Mrs Bamber shot him a quick glance. I couldn't hear her very clearly because of Gregory, and because she spoke really softly, but it sounded like she said, "We *are* meant to be having dinner."

That was when Kuba stopped shoving pieces of meat under her mashed potatoes and suddenly looked up at Mr Bamber.

"It isn't the moon," said Kuba very slowly. "It is I."

Mr Bamber looked at her for the first time. "What?"

You could tell from the expression on his face that Mr Bamber had completely forgotten that Kuba was there. I almost thought he was going to ask her who she was.

"It isn't the moon," she repeated. "It is I."

Confusion settled on Mr Bamber's face. "You?"

Kuba nodded solemnly. "Yes, exactly. I am the why."

Mrs Bamber picked up the meat platter and started waving it over the table.

"Wouldn't someone like a little more roast beef?" she asked in a chirpy voice. She smiled hopefully at her adopted daughter. "Kuba? You can't be used to meat like this where you come from."

"No." Kuba shook her head. "No, I am not. I understand that this meat is not very good for you." She smiled. "Because of the mad cows."

Mrs Bamber put the platter back down.

"Just what do you mean, *you're* the why?" demanded Mr Bamber. "What have you done to the dog?"

Mrs Bamber's smile was starting to wobble. "David, please..."

Kuba, however, was as calm as a stone.

"I have done nothing," said Kuba. "The dog, he doesn't like me." To tell you the truth, she did look a little like an angel when she smiled the way she was smiling at Mr Bamber right then. "I think he is afraid of me."

I don't think I'd ever heard Mr Bamber really laugh before. It sounded like something was breaking. I nearly dropped my book.

"Gregory? Afraid of *you*?" Mr Bamber stabbed a big chunk of beef with his fork and shook it in Kuba's direction. "I'll have you know that dog is a trained killer, young lady. He wouldn't be afraid of an armed burglar, and he certainly isn't afraid of you."

Kuba was still smiling. "How strange is the world. In my country we eat the dogs, and in your country the dogs eat the people."

"Good grief!" gasped Mrs Bamber. "Do you really eat dogs?"

"Arabella!" Mr Bamber snapped, but now he was smiling at Kuba. It looked like he'd finally remembered who she was. "So, speaking of what a strange world it is, how are you finding it here in Campton, Kuba?"

"Very different," Kuba answered politely. "I am finding it very different."

"And a little lonely," put in Mrs Bamber. "But that'll all change once school starts on Monday." She smiled encouragingly. "Then you'll have plenty of friends."

Mr Bamber leaned back in his chair.

"You know, I ran into that Blue boy on my way back from my meeting today..."

Until then I'd sort of been watching as if they were on a video, but now I sat up a little straighter.

"What's his name?" Mr Bamber was saying. "Alamo?"

"Elmo," said Mrs Bamber and me at the same time.

"Right. Elmo." Mr Bamber nodded. "Seems like a nice young man."

I couldn't help frowning at that. He certainly hadn't acted like he thought I was a nice young man that afternoon.

Mr Bamber gave Kuba an encouraging wink. "And he only lives across the road, you know. I was thinking, it doesn't matter that much that you're a girl. You could still be friends with him."

I hadn't seen Mr Bamber take out his wallet, but it was suddenly in his hand. My father's wallet is this cloth thing from Guatemala, but Mr Bamber's was leather. He slowly removed a twenty pound note and held it in the air.

"You know, Kuba, you'd be doing me a big favour if you made friends with the Blue boy. Get to know him … get invited to his house…"

Kuba looked from the money to Mr Bamber. "Excuse me? There is a *blue* boy here?"

Mr Bamber rumbled, which I took to be another of his laughs.

"No, no. *He's* not blue. Blue's his name. Alamo Blue."

"Elmo," said me and Mrs Bamber.

This very patient expression came on Kuba's face.

"The Alamo was a fort in the American West," Kuba said very sweetly to Mr Bamber.

"I believe the Texans were badly defeated there." She pushed her plate away even though I hadn't actually seen her eat anything. "Davy Crockett."

"Davy Crockett!" exclaimed Mr Bamber. "That's right! What an amazing coincidence. Davy Crockett." Mr Bamber beamed at Mrs Bamber. "She's a bright little thing, isn't she?" But he didn't give his wife a chance to actually reply. "Crosswood Cove is going to be Grace Blue's Alamo!"

"Davy Crockett was shot at the Alamo," explained Kuba. "Are you planning to shoot Grace Blue?"

"Oh, no!" gasped Mrs Bamber. "Of course he doesn't mean that. Your father would never … you don't mean that, do you David?"

Mr Bamber was huffing and puffing like the Big Bad Wolf.

"Of course I don't mean that. All I mean is that the Goofy Greeners are going to lose." The note waved back and forth between his fingers. "With a little help from our young friend from South America here."

Mr Bamber's young friend from South America wasn't even looking at him. She was politely asking Mrs Bamber if she wanted any help to clear the table.

Mr Bamber cleared his throat. "I said, 'With a little help from our young friend from South America!'" The crisp note rattled.

"No thank you, dear," Mrs Bamber said to Kuba. "Why don't you go and watch TV?"

"Just hang on a minute," said Mr Bamber. "I haven't finished talking to her yet."

Mrs Bamber got up and started clearing the table herself.

"David, please... I don't really think this is either the time or the place. I thought we could have a nice family evening." Knives and forks clattered. "And for heaven's sake, put away that money."

Mr Bamber gave her this disgusted look and turned back to Kuba. "Did you hear me?" he said. "I haven't finished talking to you yet."

And then he just sort of sat there with his mouth open.

I hadn't seen her go either.

"How the hell did she get out of here so quickly?" Mr Bamber said to himself.

Mrs Bamber too, was staring at the place where Kuba had been about half a nanosecond before, but she didn't look surprised. She was smiling.

"She's very graceful, isn't she?" said Mrs Bamber. She picked up a stack of plates. "And her English is much better than I originally thought."

I BEGIN TO REALIZE THAT I HAVE NO CHOICE

I planned to keep my distance from Kuba at school. A hundred miles would have suited me, but a couple of metres would do.

So on Monday morning I waited until I saw Mrs Bamber and Kuba drive off in Mrs Bamber's silver Porsche, and then I got my bike from the porch. I didn't want to get to school early and have to hang around with Kuba in the playground, so I took the scenic route, past the woods that Mr Bamber wanted to tear down.

My mother once rescued a fox cub she found by the side of the road there. I suppose that's the one advantage of the milk float: you can't help seeing things on the roadside because you're going so slowly. A car had hit the cub's mother.

My mother took it home and fed it till it was able to be on its own. She called it Mohican.

But even though she kept it in a run in the back garden, it gave us all fleas. Especially me.

I hadn't thought about Mohican in ages, but I thought about him as I pedalled through the woods on Monday morning. I even stopped at the place where she found him. I wondered where he was and if he had a family of his own now. I wondered where he'd go when there were tower blocks and golf carts everywhere instead of trees. Despite the fleas, I'd sort of liked Mohican. I even taught him to fetch a ball, only instead of bringing it back to me, he always dropped it in his water bowl. My mother said he was asserting his independence.

The last bell was ringing as I steamed through the school gates. I could see Kuba's hat disappearing into the building behind the other kids. I sighed with relief. This was going to be easier than I thought.

Not that I'm boasting or anything, but I'm in all the top classes. It was unlikely that they were going to put a girl from the Third World in the top classes, so all I had to hope was that we had different lunch breaks.

I was the last one into my tutor group, but nobody noticed, especially not Mr Palfry.

Mr Palfry was standing at the front of the room beside a tall girl in a long black skirt and a red blouse with mirrors all over it, and an old man's hat. He looked like he'd never seen anyone quite like her before.

Which he hadn't.

"This is Kuba Bamber," he was saying. "Kuba Bamber. She's new to our country." He smiled hopefully at Kuba. "Where in South America do you come from?"

Kuba smiled back. She was in her I-learned-my-English-from-robots mode.

"I like it here very much," she answered. "I eat mad cows and am killed by dogs."

Half of the boys nearly fell off their seats, they laughed so much.

Mr Palfry gave the class a dark look, and then smiled at Kuba again.

"What country do you come from?" he repeated. He was speaking really slowly and loudly. He sounded as if he'd learned his English from robots, too. "What country? Peru? Colombia? The Dominican Republic?"

That really patient look came over Kuba's face.

"I believe if you look on a map you will see that the Dominican Republic is not in South America," Kuba politely informed Mr Palfry. "It is an island. In the Caribbean."

Mr Palfry blinked. "Right," he mumbled. "Of course. Not the Dominican Republic."

That was when Kuba spotted me. She raised a hand in greeting. "Elmo! Good morning!"

I could've died.

Everybody turned to stare at me. Eddie

66

Kilgour stuck out his tongue. Eddie Kilgour was sort of like Richard III, or maybe the Joker in *Batman* – really clever but not exactly someone you'd want to spend too much time with. Eddie Kilgour hated my guts.

I thought Mr Palfry was going to faint with relief.

"Do you two know each other?" He looked from her to me. "Elmo, do you know Kuba?"

I slinked into my seat. "Sort of."

"Well that's great!" Mr Palfry slapped the register in his palm. "That's absolutely brilliant. I'll tell you what, Elmo, since you and Kuba are in all the same lessons and you already know each other, why don't you show her around today? Be her guide to Campton Secondary."

God might be on my mother's side, but He certainly didn't seem to be on mine.

"But Mr Palfry—"

Mr Palfry peered at me over his glasses. "But what?"

Kuba was standing there, innocent as a cherub, smiling at Mr Palfry as though she was trying very hard to understand what he was saying.

Eddie Kilgour started shaking his arm in the air.

"Mr Palfry! Mr Palfry! I'll be her guide!" He leaned over to his best mate, Bryan Ludlow, and gave him a poke. "If I play my cards right,

I'll be riding round town in a silver Porsche!" he hissed. The two of them laughed.

"Well, Eddie, that's very kind of you…" Mr Palfry hesitated. You could tell he knew that Eddie would never volunteer to do anything unless he was going to benefit personally.

If I'd thought about it rationally, I would have realized that Kuba Bamber needed my help against Eddie Kilgour about as much as a polar bear needs a winter coat, but I wasn't thinking rationally. This feeling just sort of came over me. I felt protective. Kuba was my neighbour, after all. And very foreign.

I sat up straighter. "It's all right, Mr Palfry," I called. "I'd be happy to show her round."

It wasn't too bad when we were in lessons or going to lessons, because there were so many people around. Kuba kept her hat on, smiled politely, and spoke stiffly and softly. She acted all shy and demure, just as she had with the Bambers the night before.

Neither Kuba nor I said anything about her being in my room or turning up in the high street as we trudged through the corridors together. We talked about lessons, and teachers, and stuff like that. Well, I talked about those things, and she nodded and smiled and said "Oh" and "Yes" and "No" and "Really" in her robot voice. After a while I began to think that she wasn't going to say anything about her visits. Ever. I even began to hope that the thousand signatures my mother and I'd got on Sunday meant that her mission was completed.

I should have known better than that.

Ariel Moordock and Poppy Shaw came up to us after the last lesson of the morning.

"Elmo's had you all to himself for long enough," Ariel said to Kuba. "We'd like you to eat lunch with us."

I reacted faster than an electron.

"Hey, that's a great idea. You do that. I'll meet you after lunch."

Kuba smiled and shook her head.

"Yes," she told them. "I am eating my lunch with Elmo."

"No, you don't understand," put in Poppy. "*We*–want–*you*–to–have–lunch–with–*us*." She sounded like my mother's cassette player just before it eats your tape.

Kuba smiled and nodded some more. "Thank you," she said. "Yes, Elmo and I are eating lunch."

Ariel and Poppy didn't have the stamina for this. They exchanged glances and shuffled about for a second or two.

"Yeah, right," they said. "Well, we'll see you around."

I watched them walk off with a heart that wasn't so much sinking as dropping like a rock.

"Why didn't you go with them?" I urged. "I

thought Mrs Bamber wanted you to make friends."

The smile Kuba gave me was different to the one she gave everybody else. It was more like lemon than sugar.

"What did you think of dinner with the Bambers? Was it boring, or was it boring?"

"It wasn't that boring," I heard myself say. "There were a couple of pretty interesting bits."

The lemon content of her smile increased, but all she said was, "Let's find somewhere quiet to have our lunch. You and I need to talk."

"Can't you talk to someone else?" I pleaded. "I'm feeling very stressed out at the moment."

"You?" hooted Kuba. "How do you think *I* feel? I'm the one being fed dead cow."

She turned on her heel and started walking towards the cafeteria, as if *she* were showing *me* round.

I was more like my mother than I cared to admit. I had instincts, too. My instincts were telling me that it was no use trying to sneak away. I was doomed.

Feeling like the condemned prisoner being led to the electric chair, I followed Kuba to an empty corner of the cafeteria.

"So, how many signatures did you get yesterday?" Kuba asked me as soon as we sat down.

"A thousand." I didn't tell her that my mother thought it was a miracle.

"Is that enough?" Mrs Bamber had given Kuba money for a hot dinner, but she'd got a couple of apples and a salad instead. She bit into an apple. "You only have three days left to make up for the missing signatures. The Council meets on Thursday."

As if I didn't know. I was the one who was being forced to pound the streets for the next three days. My mother was so encouraged by how well we did yesterday – especially by how well *I* did – that she had almost taken me out of school for a couple of days so I could put more time in. I'd had to make up an important science test to stop her.

I unwrapped my sandwich. "I know when the Council meets," I said sourly.

Kuba acted as if I hadn't said anything.

"Well?" she persisted. "Do you have enough?"

I sniffed at my sandwich. I was sure I could smell seaweed.

"I have no idea," I lied. I didn't want her helping any more.

"You're lying," said Kuba. She didn't say it like an accusation, but just as a statement of fact. There was no point arguing.

"I don't think so," I admitted grudgingly. "But we have got three days."

"I think I can help," said Kuba.

I gave her a look out of the corner of my eye. "You're not meant to interfere, remember?"

"It's not really interfering," said Kuba. "I just want to show you something."

Hadn't she shown me enough? I gave her another look. "Show me what?"

She smiled down at me. "Oh, just something."

"I don't have time for your tricks," I informed her coldly. "I've got to go to the library before our next lesson. My mother's collecting me straight after school." And parking the milk float two blocks away. "We're doing that new super supermarket today."

Kuba put down her apple.

"I know," she said. "But this won't take a minute."

"I just want to eat my lunch and then go to the library," I protested.

"Less than one minute," said Kuba, and she thrust an open notebook in front of me.

It was just an ordinary, spiral-bound notebook. It was open at a blank page.

"What's this?"

"Look," ordered Kuba. "You're not looking."

I looked at the notebook.

What had been a blank page a nanosecond ago was now a photograph of Mr Bamber, driving along in his car. Except, of course, that it wasn't exactly a photograph, it was more like a video, because Mr Bamber really was driving. He pulled into the car park by the new super supermarket. He didn't park, though; he drove round the back.

I tried not to let my jaw drop as I watched Mr Bamber stop his car and get out. He had his mobile phone in his coat pocket and his briefcase in his hand. He kept looking over his shoulder.

"What is this?" I whispered.

"Just look," said Kuba.

Mr Bamber strolled over to the row of enormous metal bins where the supermarket rubbish was put. He looked over his shoulder a couple more times, and then he opened his briefcase and took out a large brown envelope. There was a green and white Keep Our Planet Green label on the front and the word "Petition" printed across it. Mr Bamber stood on his toes and chucked the envelope into the air. It fell into the nearest bin. Mr Bamber smiled, snapped his briefcase shut, and strolled back to his car.

I turned to Kuba.

Aghast is another of my grandmother's words. I was definitely feeling aghast.

"But that's the envelope Mrs Ludgate lost!"

"I know." Kuba shut the notebook and stuck it back in her schoolbag.

For somebody who was determined to help

whether I wanted her to or not, she could be incredibly unhelpful when she put her mind to it.

"Well, what am I supposed to do now?"

Kuba shrugged. "That's up to you." She jabbed her fork in her salad. "I'm afraid that I can't interfere."

All the way to the new super supermarket, I thought about what I'd seen in Kuba's notebook. The only thing I felt really sure about at the moment was the fact that whenever Kuba even vaguely suggested something, I ended up doing it.

But not this time. There was no way I was crawling into some disgusting dustbin to see if the Greeners' envelope was really in it. Not if an army of angels moved into my road.

We must have had a tail wind behind us or something, because before I knew it my mother was parking the milk float in a space near the shops.

She turned off the ignition and looked at her watch. She gave it a shake.

"Maybe it's not as far as I thought..." she mumbled. Then she looked over at me. "We've made such good time. Maybe it's a sign that God is smiling down on us again."

"Yeah," I said. Or laughing.

My mother was going to station herself in front of the super supermarket itself. I was to

74

take up my post by the garden centre. She gave me a bright smile and handed me my clipboard. She wished me luck. I wished her luck, too. I reckoned we would both need it.

It was a beautiful September afternoon, sunny and warm. Not only had about half the county picked that afternoon as their day to do their shopping or buy some new plants, but most of them seemed eager to sign my petition. A woman with lots of little kids all screaming around her even said I was a "fine young man".

"What a fine young man," she said, "doing something worthwhile instead of sitting at home watching television."

I forced myself to smile. With Kuba living across the road, I might never watch telly again.

After a couple of hours the crowds began to thin out. It was getting near the time we'd have to leave if we wanted to get home for supper, and I found myself wondering if maybe I shouldn't just have a look behind the shop. You know, to see if it looked in real life like it did in Kuba's notebook.

I looked over at my mother. A bus full of women with shopping bags was unloading in front of the supermarket, and my mother was at the door, grabbing people as they tried to get off.

I glanced around at the garden centre. No

one coming out or going in. I did another check on my mother. Her back was to me now. Why not? I decided. Taking one quick look couldn't hurt.

I stuck my clipboard behind a tree and ran around the corner.

It didn't really come as any great surprise that the back of the super supermarket looked just like it did in Kuba's notebook. Except, of course, that Mr Bamber's BMW wasn't parked there any more.

There were four bins in a row. I stood where I thought the car had been, trying to work out which bin Mr Bamber had chucked the envelope in.

It's that one, I decided. The second from the left.

And then I gave myself a shake. What was I thinking of? The bins weren't the kind you put out at the front of the house; they were gigantic. Mr Bamber had stood on his toes to reach the bin; I'd have to be on stilts.

"This is ridiculous," I scolded myself. "Kuba's playing games, and you know it. Go back to your post."

But even while I was saying that stuff to myself I was looking round for a ladder. Not that there was one.

"That's it," I said. "I'm going back to the garden centre."

And then I saw some largish wooden crates,

76

stacked beside a door.

"I'll just see if there's anything right on the top," I told myself as I lugged a crate over to the nearest bin. "If I don't I'll be thinking about it all night."

Standing on the crate, my eyebrows reached the top of the bin. I stood on my toes. Now I could see *over* the bin, but I still couldn't see in.

I reckoned there was nothing more I could do. I'm not an athlete. When we play rounders and stuff like that at school, I'm always the last one picked because no one wants me on their team. There was no way I was going to even try to heave myself over the rim.

The door where the crates were stacked groaned open.

I looked over. A shoe, a hand and a newspaper appeared in the crack. I could hear men's voices.

I stopped thinking completely then. Terror can make you stronger than you usually are, I've seen it in films. And I was definitely terrified. The last thing I wanted was to be caught hanging off a dustbin at the back of the supermarket. Not by those men at the door, and not by Grace Blue. My instincts took over again. Endowed for a moment with superhuman strength, I pulled myself up and over, landing flat on my face on top of the rubbish.

I nearly cried out loud. I was lying on a pile

of rotten fruit that smelled like Gertie after she pukes.

The men were having a break. I could hear them talking about the coffee machine and what time the football was on that night. They dragged out a couple of crates to sit on.

I got to my feet and cautiously peered over the edge of the bin.

Two men were sitting against the building, drinking soft drinks. One of them had a newspaper and the other one was reading it with him over his shoulder. They had no idea I was there.

Trying not to make a sound, and almost gagging, I climbed into the next bin. I should have looked first.

You know that bit in *Alice in Wonderland* when she falls down the rabbit hole?

Well that's what it felt like. The first bin was full to the top, but the second bin wasn't. It was hardly full at all.

I stood up. By standing on my toes, I could just touch the top edge of the bin. But I didn't have enough grip to even pretend to pull myself up.

Suddenly, I was really angry with Kuba. What was the use of being friends with someone who said she was an angel if she was never around when you *really* needed her?

"Elmo? Elmo?"

I froze. It was my mother. She was looking

for me.

"Elmo? Elmo, where are you?"

One of the men asked her what was wrong.

My mother told him about the petition and that she'd seen me running towards the back of the shop. She said she thought I must be looking for a toilet.

"Well, there's no loo back here," said the second man.

"He must have gone into the garden centre," my mother decided. I heard her start to walk away.

I had two choices: stay where I was till everyone had gone or shout for help.

If I waited till everyone had gone I might not get out of the bin until the dustmen came. By then my mother would have discovered that I wasn't in the garden centre, or in the super supermarket, and she would have called the police.

If I shouted for help the men and my mother could get me out straight away and I could go home and forget the whole thing had happened.

It was the thought of being driven home in a police car that made up my mind. I shouted. Loud and clear.

"Mum? Mum, I'm in here!"

My mother's footsteps stopped.

"Elmo?"

I started jumping up and down. "In here,

Mum! In here!"

The man who had asked my mother what was wrong said, "He's in the dustbin!"

They decided to tip the bin gently on to its side.

"All right!" called the men. "On the count of three."

My mother did the counting. "One ... two ... three..."

The bin banged on the ground and I tumbled out with a whole load of rubbish.

The men reached down and helped me to my feet.

"Are you all right?" asked one.

"How on earth did you get in there?" asked the other.

My mother started to say something comforting but she stopped after, "Oh, Elmo..." She furrowed her brow and stooped to pick something up. "What's this?"

The men and I looked at what she was holding in her hands. The men didn't say anything because they didn't know what it was. I didn't say anything because I did.

She was holding the Greeners' envelope with the word "Petition" written on the front.

MR BAMBER SNATCHES VICTORY FROM THE JAWS OF DEFEAT

My mother called an emergency meeting of the Greeners on Tuesday to tell them about finding the missing petitions.

"I don't know why you need a meeting," grumbled my father. A meeting meant that Gertie would be helping him in his studio until she was ready for bed. "They all know already."

My mother had been on the phone most of Monday night telling them.

"We have our strategy to plan, as well," said my mother. "We don't want to lose the petitions again."

My father took two home-made biscuits from the plate on the table. It was still a little early for a victory celebration, but my mother was in a party mood.

"Just don't let Caroline Ludgate near them," was my father's advice. "She'd forget her head if it wasn't firmly attached."

"I'm not so sure it was Caroline's fault," said my mother.

"Really?" said my father. "Are you forgetting the time she left Barry at the shopping centre?"

Barry was Mrs Ludgate's son. He was a plumber now, but at the time he'd been a little boy. She didn't even realize he was missing until he phoned for her to come back and get him.

"It's easy enough to misplace a child," said my mother. "This is different. I'm beginning to think that someone deliberately took them."

My father choked on his biscuit. "I don't think petty thievery is Mr Bamber's style, Grace." He winked. "It might mess up his suit."

"But he could get someone else to do it," argued my mother.

My father shook his head.

"I don't think so, love. Even Old Building Breath wouldn't stoop that low."

I didn't get involved because I reckoned that it didn't really matter. My mother was happy because she was sure the Council would side with the Greeners on Thursday, but I was even happier. I didn't have to stand on any more street corners.

My father gave Gertie a piece of biscuit. "What I still don't understand is what Elmo

82

was doing in the dustbin," said my father.

"I told you," said my mother. She gave me a big smile. "He was rescuing a cat."

My father removed his finger from Gertie's mouth and looked at me. "You? Since when have *you* been interested in animals?"

This was a valid point. Because my mother brings home any stray animal she finds, especially if it's bleeding, we'd had everything from an escaped parrot to the baby fox. The parrot bit me. You already know about the fleas. I'd sort of officially gone off animals after that.

My mother said, "Fuller, please. Who cares? Elmo's safe and the petitions are safe ... thank God he went into that dustbin, that's what I say." She got this soppy look on her face. "It really is a miracle. I mean, what are the chances of that happening?"

About ten billion to one, was my guess.

My father said, "About the same as Elmo risking his life for a cat."

My mother laughed as if she thought he was joking.

"Well, all I know is that Elmo's saved the day. Mr Bamber doesn't stand a chance against us now."

"What a relief," I said.

Which it was. Now Kuba would leave me alone.

Because my mother was so grateful to me

for the part I'd played in finding the missing signatures, she invited me to join her and the other Greeners when they presented the petitions to the Council on Thursday morning.

"After all," said my mother, "you're the hero of the hour. You have to be there for our moment of triumph."

Normally the idea of going anywhere with the Greeners filled me with horror. They were unreliable companions for a small child because you could never be sure when something was going to upset them and they were going to start a fight. My own mother had once humiliated me so much by lecturing a woman in the shopping centre about wearing a fur coat that I locked myself in my room for a whole day. But to tell you the truth, I was pretty chuffed about finding the petitions for her, and I was pleased that she'd asked me to go to a meeting that was so important. It sort of made me feel like I was taller than I really was.

"I'll be there," I promised. "Wild horses couldn't keep me away."

"Me neither," said my mother.

On Thursday my mother wrote a note for me so I could get out of lessons. Because my school wasn't far from where the Council meeting was being held, my mother was going to meet me at the main door at 11 a.m.

I was dead on time.

I reckoned the rest of the Greeners and Mr Bamber and his lot must have gone straight in, because there was no one hanging around outside. I chained my bike to the railing and sat down on the steps to wait for my mother.

At about eleven-fifteen, I stood up, walked to the middle of the pavement and looked as hard as I could in both directions. There was a familiar-looking red blur coming from the left.

I waved.

The blur waved back.

"Hurry up!" I called. "They're going to start without us."

"Where's your mother?" asked the red blur.

Only it wasn't a red blur any more; it was Kuba. I didn't want to believe it. I took off my glasses, rubbed them on my shirt and put them back on. It really was Kuba.

"What are you doing here?" I demanded. "How did you get out of school?"

"I've got a dentist's appointment." Kuba pointed down the road. "I have to come past here to get there."

I nearly laughed with relief. For one terrible minute I'd thought she was up to something.

"Oh," I said, not trying too hard to hide my happiness. "My mother's not here yet."

"I thought the meeting started at eleven-thirty," said Kuba.

I scowled. I hated the way she always knew everything.

"We still have fifteen minutes," I said sourly. "Something must have held her up." I looked up and down the road again, but there was no sign of Grace Blue and her bicycle.

Kuba took hold of my arm. "Come on," she said, "I think you and I should go for a ride."

"A ride? Are you mad? I thought you had a dentist's appointment."

Kuba shrugged. "Mrs Bamber made a mistake, the appointment is for tomorrow." She smiled brightly. "So we've got time for a little ride."

I stood up as tall as was possible for me and looked her in the eye. "For the last time, will you just leave me alone? I want you to stop helping me."

The bright smile turned sour.

"That's gratitude for you. If it weren't for me you wouldn't have found the petitions."

"If it weren't for you I wouldn't have been up to my waist in rubbish."

She made a face. "That's what *you* say."

"Yes, that is what I say. I don't know why I had to go through all that when you could have told me exactly what bin they were in."

She sighed impatiently. "Because if I *told* you it would be interfering, that's why. Some things you have to discover for yourself."

"Right," I said. "And now I'm waiting for

my mother by myself."

"We can ride while you wait," said Kuba.

I had no intention of going for a ride with Kuba, then or ever. And I told her so.

"We're not going anywhere," I told her firmly. "My mother's expecting to meet me right here. And here is where I'm going to be. Besides, you don't have a bike."

"I don't need one," said Kuba. "I'll ride on your crossbar."

I was a bit surprised to realize that, while I was telling Kuba very firmly that I wasn't going anywhere, my bike had somehow found its way to where I was standing and I was already climbing on.

I gave Kuba my sternest look.

"We're only going once round the block, right?"

"Right," said Kuba. "Once round the block."

I have a very vivid memory of holding the bike steady while Kuba slipped on to the crossbar. She was big, but she was unexpectedly light, which was a bit of a blessing.

"I wish you were shorter," I complained. "It's hard to see where we're going."

"Don't worry." Kuba rang the bell. "You'll be fine."

I also have a very vivid memory of pushing off, and wobbling as I slowly pedalled to the corner.

"Are you sure you can't see her coming?"

Kuba nodded. "I couldn't be surer."

When we reached the corner, I carefully turned into Pembroke Road.

So far so good.

But that was as far as the good went. And that's all I remember that followed the rules of the real world.

I was the only person except for the Greeners who knew the secret route my mother was taking that morning. At least I was *meant* to be the only person. But obviously I wasn't.

I turned into Pembroke Road, but it wasn't Pembroke Road that lay ahead of us. It was the back road that ran from behind our house into town. I recognized the field of cows and the huddle of trees just before the bend.

I wanted to turn round. Wanted to? I'd have given away my computer to turn round. But I couldn't. It was as if my bike was attached to an invisible rope that kept pulling it along no matter which way I turned. I wasn't even really pedalling; it was more like the pedals were moving my feet.

"I want to go back!" I shouted to Kuba. "Make us go back!"

Kuba shook her head and her hair flew between us like a scarf. "Isn't this fun?" she cried happily. "I haven't done this for decades."

"Well, I wish you hadn't picked now," I

screamed. The brakes weren't working, either.

We passed the cows and the trees and turned into the bend.

I started to repeat my wish to go back, but I got no further than "I want". The words disappeared from my mouth.

Just ahead of us, my mother's bike was lying at the side of the road, its front wheel twisted and the trailer on its side in the ditch. Dozens of sheets of paper were scattered along the hedgerow like weird flowers. My mother was picking them up.

She stopped when she spotted me and Kuba steaming towards her.

"Elmo!" She came running over to us. In twelve years, I'd never seen her so happy to see me before. "Thank God you're here!" She was so happy that she didn't even ask us *why* we were there.

We screeched to a halt.

"What happened? Were you hit by a car?"

My mother looked a bit wild-eyed and shocked. She pushed a strand of hair from her face.

"You're not going to believe this," said my mother, "but it was horses. They came out of nowhere."

She was riding along, thinking about the meeting, when she suddenly saw two horses charging down the road towards her.

"They must have been runaways from one

of the farms. I thought they'd break apart when they got closer to me, but if that was what they intended to do they left it too late."

My mother swerved to miss them and landed in the hedge. The petitions were in two cardboard boxes that weren't as secure as they should have been. When the trailer toppled over, the petitions all went flying.

"It's almost as if they were waiting for me round that bend," my mother said. "One minute they weren't there, and the next minute they were. I didn't have time to stop."

My mother and I picked up the rest of the petitions while Kuba stayed at the side of the road and examined my mother's bike with a serious expression.

"It's fine now," said Kuba when we came back. She moved the front wheel back and forth. "See? It was just a little bent."

"Elmo," said my mother. "Aren't you going to introduce me to your friend?"

As if I had a choice.

"Mum," I said, "this is Kuba. Kuba, this is my mother." I gave my mother a little nudge. "Shouldn't you be getting into town? The meeting's star—"

My mother gave me a curious look.

"I've been wanting to meet you for ages," said Kuba. "But Elmo wasn't really keen."

I could have kicked her. As if she'd been begging me to introduce her to my mother! As if what I wanted counted for anything!

"You really are a strange child, aren't you?" said my mother.

It took me a second to realize that she wasn't talking to Kuba.

"It isn't that nonsense about you living with the Bambers, is it?" my mother was saying to Kuba. "Because I told Elmo that you're welcome in our home any time you like."

"I'm so glad to hear that!" Kuba gave my mother a hug. "Really. I can't tell you how happy that makes me."

And I couldn't tell her how unhappy it made *me*.

"So how are you getting on?" asked my mother. "Are you settling in all right?"

Kuba shrugged. "So-so. Mrs Bamber is very nice, but Mr Bamber is very busy."

"Yeah," said my mother, "busy destroying the planet."

My mother took Kuba and the petitions in the trailer and I followed on my bike. Kuba sat facing me, but she rested her head on her arms so that all I could see was the top of her hat.

And on the top of her hat I could see the Council meeting. It had already begun.

The Council meeting was being held in a large, high room with old photographs of historic Campton on the walls. There was an enormous wooden table in the centre of the room that took up most of the floor space. Sitting round the table were the members of Campton Council, the Executive Committee of Keep Our Planet Green (Mr Meadows and Mrs Ludgate), and Mr Bamber and a couple of other people in expensive suits with briefcases and mobile phones.

The image was so clear I almost felt as though I was sitting at the table, too. Or I would have if the wind hadn't been blowing my head back because we were going so fast. I couldn't help wondering if television had actually been invented by angels. They obviously had it first.

The members of the Council were sipping water and tapping their pens on the table. The chairman of the Council was looking at his watch.

Mr Bamber cleared his throat.

"This is preposterous," said Mr Bamber. He smiled almost sadly. "We're busy people. And time, after all, is money."

Mr Meadows said, "We have to wait for Mrs Blue. She'll be here shortly. She must have been delayed."

The chairman looked at his watch again.

"We've already been here half an hour," he said. "The Council does have other things on its agenda."

"But that's not fair!" Mrs Ludgate was another person who knew what it meant to feel aghast. "We were told the meeting was to begin at eleven-thirty, not eleven. Grace is only a few minutes late."

One of the councillors, Mrs Marklew, looked up from doodling on the pad in front of her to raise an eyebrow in Mrs Ludgate's direction.

"You were told eleven o'clock, just as the rest of us were." She said it in the way God might have reminded Adam that he knew he wasn't meant to eat that apple.

Mrs Ludgate spluttered, but whatever she was trying to say was drowned out by Mr Bamber.

"Mr Chairman," said Mr Bamber, "with all due respect, if I might remind the members of the Council, my firm has complied with every regulation *and* has the full support of the Chamber of Commerce as well as most of the local residents."

"Not quite *most* of the local residents," Mr Meadows corrected. He turned to the members of the Council. They looked as if they were trying not to yawn. "When Mrs Blue arrives with our petitions, you'll see for yourselves just how many local residents are in favour of Mr Bamber's proposal."

Mr Bamber laughed. "This meeting was already cancelled once because of these mythical petitions of yours." He smiled knowingly at the chairman of the Council. "If you want my personal opinion, I shouldn't think they have enough signatures to get them into a charity walk."

Everyone except Mr Meadows and Mrs Ludgate chuckled over that.

"That's not true!" cried Mrs Ludgate. "We have thousands. We—"

"*Lost* them all is what I heard," cut in Mr Bamber. He didn't sound like he believed her. "But even if you *did* have them and lost them, I find it difficult to believe that you've made up for them in a week."

"But we did!" Mrs Ludgate protested. "We found them again!"

"Found them again?" Mr Bamber gave her a you-poor-mad-thing sort of look. Then he turned to the chairman with another knowing smile. "It's all a little too convenient, if you ask me."

"I agree with David," said the man on Mr Bamber's right. "If you ask me, this whole thing is just a stalling tactic."

The man on Mr Bamber's left snapped his briefcase closed. "I'm afraid I have to be in court in an hour," he informed the Council. "Either we continue with the meeting or I'll have to leave."

I was still staring at the top of Kuba's head as we pulled up in front of the Council building. She was back to wearing just an old felt hat.

My mother blinked and looked at her watch.

"Goodness me," she murmured, "I feel as though I've been asleep or something. I can't remember how we got here so fast."

I wasn't going to be the one to tell her. I looked at Kuba.

Kuba smiled. "I think you should step on it." She gave my mother a gentle shove.

My mother immediately stopped being curious about how it took us less than a minute to ride three miles and grabbed the box Kuba was handing her.

"You're right," she said. "Come on, Elmo. We have a meeting to attend."

If we'd been in a film, my mother and I would have raced into the building and thundered through reception and up the stairs to where the Council was meeting on the second floor. Clerks and secretaries would have pressed themselves against the walls to let us pass. At last we would have reached the door we wanted. We'd have heard angry voices coming from inside. Mr Bamber would have been shouting. "I move that the Council votes now." Mrs Ludgate would have been pleading, "Mrs Blue is on her way. Just give us a few more minutes." That was when my mother and I would have burst triumphantly through the door with the petitions in our arms. The Council would finally have understood how many people were against Mr Bamber's houses and they'd have refused him permission. Everyone but Mr Bamber would have cheered. My mother and I would have had tears in our eyes.

With a wave to Kuba, my mother and I locked up our bikes and hurried inside. We didn't have time to wait for the lift; we ran.

"We can still make it," my mother kept mumbling as we pounded up the stairs. "We can still make it."

Up until that point, what happened was pretty much what would have happened if we had been in a film.

But when we got to the second floor Mrs Ludgate and Mr Meadows were sitting on a wooden bench in the corridor and the meeting room was empty.

"What happened?" shrieked my mother.

Mrs Ludgate and Mr Meadows gazed back at her with stunned expressions.

"We were going to ask you the very same thing," said Mr Meadows.

To say that my mother was disappointed would be like saying you might get a little damp if you fell into the sea. My mother was beside herself with anger and frustration.

"But why didn't they wait?" she wailed. Her eyes darted from Mrs Ludgate to Mr Meadows and back again. "Didn't you tell them I had the petitions? Why didn't they wait?"

"Of course we told them," said Mrs Ludgate indignantly. "But Mr Bamber convinced them that we were stalling." She moistened her lips and avoided my mother's eyes. "He seemed to know about the signatures I lost," she went on softly. "Nobody believed we'd found them again."

Mr Meadows patted my mother's shoulder. "Don't worry, Grace," he said. "Tomorrow is another day. I'm sure we'll have another chance to come up against Mr Bamber, and next time we'll win."

My mother may have been defeated, but she was far from being beaten.

"And who said I had finished with him this time?" asked my mother.

SHERLOCK HOLMES IN CAMPTON

I avoided Kuba for the rest of the day, and for a change she didn't just stroll into my room demanding to talk. My mother's defeat upset me more than I thought it would and, weird as it may sound, I blamed Kuba. She was the angel. Why didn't she get us there on time?

But on Friday afternoon, as I was unlocking my bike, Kuba suddenly appeared at my side in the school playground. I flatly refused to give her a ride home.

"Suit yourself," said Kuba. "We'll walk."

I smiled very sweetly. "You mean *you'll* walk. I'm cycling."

Only I couldn't get on my bike. Every time I put my foot on the pedal it slipped off.

Kuba's smile was even sweeter than mine. "Going my way?" she asked.

Neither of us spoke until we were outside school.

"Mr Bamber was beside himself last night," said Kuba. "He actually danced Mrs Bamber around the living-room, he was so happy." She rolled her eyes. "I've never seen him touch her before."

I didn't say anything. I thought of what Mrs Ludgate had said at the meeting: it was really unfair.

"How did your mother take it?" asked Kuba.

"How do you think she took it?" I snapped. "She threw a party, she was so pleased."

Kuba swung her schoolbag dangerously close to me.

"I don't know why you're angry with me," she said. "I did everything I could."

I stopped walking. "Did you?" I asked sarcastically. "Then why didn't you stop those horses? Why didn't you make sure my mother got to the meeting on time?"

Kuba's schoolbag scraped my knee.

"I'm an angel," said Kuba. "Not a magician."

I pointed out that she could turn an old hat into a television. "Seems like magic to me."

"And Mr Bamber *seems* like a nice guy," replied Kuba. She glared at me sourly. "There are limits to what I can do, Elmo. I can see things *when* they happen and *after* they happen, but not before. And I can't personally stop them from happening. That's considered interfering." Her glare became a little less sour. "But I can point others in the right direction."

I wasn't sure why, but I got the feeling that this last statement was a criticism of me. As if Kuba had pointed me in the right direction and I had refused to go. As if everything were my fault and not hers.

"Yeah, well…" I mumbled. "It doesn't seem to have done much good this time, does it?"

"This time isn't over yet," said Kuba.

My mother didn't think this time was over yet, either.

My mother had a new plan. She had tried to go through the proper channels in a proper way, but now, she said, the Greeners had to take things into their own hands.

"That's what terrorists say," said my grandfather.

My mother scowled. "I was thinking of the tactics of Gandhi, not the IRA," she said.

My mother wasn't into violence. To her, the Greeners taking things into their own hands meant bringing national attention to what was happening in Campton. Which meant that Grace Blue was prepared to sit in front of an oncoming bulldozer and chain herself to it if she had to. With her petitions firmly clasped in her arms, of course. When the police and the photographers and members of the Council turned up, my mother was going to present the petitions on the evening news. Let the country decide, said my mother.

In the meantime, Mr Bamber, confident that my mother was finally beaten, announced the day his project would start. If he didn't waste any more time, he could have the woods levelled, the lake drained and the cemetery moved before winter came and the ground was too hard. The bulldozers would be moving in on Monday.

On Friday night my mother called a special meeting of the Greeners. There were maps and signs all over the dining-room table. The living-room had been turned into a training camp. My father shut himself in his studio with Gertie, my grandparents shut themselves in their studio with their tango class, and my aunt and uncle shut themselves in their studio with a bottle of wine. I didn't have a studio, so I got myself some supper and went to my room.

Kuba was stretched out on my bed with my library book.

I knew from biology that a species' survival depends on its ability to adapt to changing conditions, but I wasn't sure I'd ever seen that principle in action before now. I, however, was like a species that is determined to survive. Just a few short days ago I'd been shocked to find Kuba in my room, but now I barely glanced at her. I locked the door behind me. It wasn't as if Kuba needed to use it, and I didn't want my mother suddenly barging in.

I pulled the chair out from under my desk. "What are you doing here?" I asked as I sat down.

"I'm reading Sherlock Holmes," said Kuba. She rested the open book on her stomach and sighed. "It's a shame he wasn't a real person," she went on almost wistfully. "We could use Mr Holmes's analytical skills."

I laughed. "Even if he had been real he'd be dead by now," I pointed out.

"You mean like me?" asked Kuba.

This was one avenue of conversation that I didn't really want to go down. If Kuba could call up other spirits I, for one, didn't want to know about it. I was still trying to adapt to all the other things she could do.

I bit into my sandwich.

Something crashed in the living-room. The Greeners were practising being dragged away by the police.

"You have to admire your mother's spirit, don't you?" she asked.

I moved my salad out of her reach.

"You mean because she doesn't know when to give up?"

"She shouldn't have to give up," said Kuba. "She should have won." She frowned. "I wonder how Mr Bamber knew…"

102

"Knew what?"

Kuba sighed. As far as angels go, patience wasn't her biggest virtue.

"Knew that she found the petitions. You don't think those runaway horses were an accident, do you?"

I stared at her. Aghast was becoming one of my favourite emotions.

"Weren't they?"

She gave me a look of exasperation. "Of course they weren't. Somebody must have told Mr Bamber that you found the petitions, and what route your mother was taking to the meeting. The question is: who?"

I put my salad back within her reach. I didn't feel like eating any more. To tell the truth, I was finding the whole thing pretty depressing. I'd really looked up to Mr Bamber. But I was beginning to feel that I'd have to lie flat on my back to look up to Mr Bamber now. I thought about this for a few minutes.

"But if somebody told Mr Bamber," I said slowly, "it had to be one of the Greeners. Nobody else knew."

Kuba's smile wasn't particularly angelic.

"Exactly." Having finished my salad, she moved on to my unfinished sandwich.

"You mean there's an informer?"

"Is the manatee nearly extinct?" asked Kuba.

I felt sort of like the way I'd felt when my

father accidentally whacked me on the head with a piece of pipe from one of his fountains. I was stunned. This wasn't just spying, this was betrayal. The hard core of Greeners had all been in the group since it began. They were my mother's friends. For her birthday they'd made her a carrot cake and adopted a tree in her name. But one of them was telling Mr Bamber the Greeners' inside secrets.

"Maybe it wasn't a coincidence that Mrs Ludgate was in charge of those petitions..." I mumbled, thinking out loud. "Maybe they were Mr Meadows' horses that ran my mother off the road..."

"I wouldn't go jumping to any conclusions," said Kuba through a mouthful of bread and hummus. "It could be anybody. It could even be someone who's close to a Greener but isn't actually in the group. A neighbour ... a friend ... even a relative..."

"Well, that narrows it down." I handed her my packet of crisps. She'd had everything else, she might as well have those, too. "We've got to do something," I said. "We've got to tell my mother."

"Tell her what?" asked Kuba. She opened the crisps. "If we tell her, she has two choices: to tell the Greeners, which means Mr Bamber will know that *we* know; or not tell them and act like nothing's wrong, which means that Mr Bamber will still know all their plans." She

104

stuffed a couple of crisps in her mouth. "Either way, he wins."

"Then we should tell her," I decided. "She might as well know she's really lost."

"She hasn't really lost," said Kuba.

I watched the last of my crisps disappear into her mouth. "But you said—"

"No, I didn't," said Kuba, crunching. "I was merely explaining why we should keep your mum and the Greeners out of our plans."

"I didn't know that we had plans," I said acidly.

"Of course we have," said Kuba. "We're going to catch Mr Bamber in his own trap."

"Oh, really? And how are we going to do that?"

"The first thing we're going to do is find out who the informer is."

"And how are we going to do that?"

"Sherlock Holmes," said Kuba.

"Excuse me?"

"Mr Bamber's up to something." She brushed crisp crumbs from her hands. "He was supposed to go out to dinner with me and Mrs Bamber and now he says he can't." The blue glow on her head was darker than usual. It made her look very serious. "He says he's got to stay at home to wait for an important phone call."

"Well, that makes sense. Mr Bamber's an important man."

Kuba tilted her head expectantly. "And?"

I got an image of Mr Bamber in my mind. Cal and Lucille called Mr Bamber the human phonebox.

"And what about his mobile?"

"Exactly, my dear Elmo," said Kuba. "What about his mobile? That man takes important calls in the loo. Why wouldn't he take one in the restaurant?"

It was beginning to look like I was Watson and Kuba was Sherlock Holmes.

"Because it's secret?"

One eyebrow rose.

"From whom? Mrs Bamber?" The blue that hovered around her head grew even darker. "What do you think Mr Bamber's doing that he can't tell Mrs Bamber?"

I watched enough telly to be able to find a logical answer to that.

"Maybe he has a girlfriend."

Kuba spluttered with laughter. "Yeah, right. But her name happens to be Stocks and Bonds."

So maybe it wasn't that logical.

"Well, there's nothing we can do about it," I said with some relief.

"There's certainly nothing I can do about it," said Kuba. "I've got to go and eat some poor dead animal in that new rainforest restaurant." She got to her feet with a sigh. "Apparently it has parrots flying around pooping on your food. Mrs Bamber seems to think I'll get a kick out of it." She sighed again. "This really is a strange world. You destroy the rainforests and then you open restaurants that recreate the rainforests. Why don't you just leave them where they are and go there for picnics?"

About ten minutes after Mrs Bamber and Kuba had driven off in the Porsche to eat some poor dead animal while parrots pooped on their plates, Mr Bamber left the house. He had Gregory with him.

I watched them stand on the front porch for a few seconds while Mr Bamber locked the door, and then they strolled down the path as though this were something they did every evening, a man and his dog out for a walk.

I wouldn't have thought anything of it if it weren't for the fact that I'd never seen Mr Bamber walk Gregory before. Not once. He was always too busy.

I blame Sherlock Holmes. Instead of getting out my homework, I grabbed my jacket from the back of the door and raced downstairs. Another example of instinct over reason.

My father was in his studio, as usual. My grandparents were in the living-room, watching a dance programme on the telly. Uncle Cal and Aunt Lucille were playing a heated game of backgammon in the kitchen. My mother was glued to the telephone in her office. No one noticed me leave the house.

Mr Bamber and Gregory were turning the corner as I reached the road.

Because we're miles out of town, there aren't many other houses near us, just woods and fields. Careful not to make any noise, I followed Mr Bamber and Gregory, keeping close to the shrubs at the side of the road. It was still pretty light out, so my problem was to make sure Mr Bamber didn't spot me.

I'd never really seen Mr Bamber walk very much before. He was always getting out of a car, or getting into a car. But that night he and Gregory walked for miles.

First, they went up by the woods that were going to be turned into a housing development. Gregory ran after a couple of rabbits and Mr Bamber smoked a cigar.

Then they cut across to the old church. It wasn't used any more, but in the summer there were always a few tourists stumbling around it, taking pictures. Gregory chased a couple of rabbits through the cemetery and Mr Bamber looked at headstones.

After that, they crossed to the lake. Mr Bamber smoked another cigar and Gregory chased a couple of ducks.

Holmes was always excited when he followed someone, but I was dead bored. I should've stayed at home and done my homework. Mr Bamber wasn't up to something. He wasn't being secretive and devious. All he was doing was taking a last look at his land before it became a golf course.

After the lake, the three of us headed back by a different road.

It was starting to get dark by then and I stopped really paying attention to where we were going.

Mr Bamber was already opening a door before I realized that we'd come to a pub. I came to a halt and watched Mr Bamber and Gregory disappear inside.

Maybe this is it, I thought. Maybe Mr Bamber's meeting someone in the pub.

Crouching low, I scuttled across the car park and up to the shrubs by the front window. It was an old building, so the windows were low. I could peek in without standing up.

Mr Bamber was standing at the bar with Gregory. There were several other men at the bar, and a few couples and a group of men at the tables around it. I recognized a few of the local farmers, and Dr Paley, the vet. Dr Paley leaned down and rubbed Gregory behind the ear, but he didn't say anything to Mr Bamber. Nobody said anything to Mr Bamber. The farmers were talking to each other, and Dr Paley was talking to the barman.

It didn't look like Mr Bamber had gone in

to meet someone. It looked like he'd gone in to have a drink.

It was only the thought of all the hours Sherlock Holmes spent watching suspects that kept me at the window. Watching people drink isn't the most exciting thing in the world, though. They talked, they laughed, they shouted a bit. One of the farmers tripped over Gregory and spilled some of his drink.

I was trying to work out if there was anything suspicious about the spilled drink or not when one of the men from the group at the table got up for another round.

He worked himself into the space between Mr Bamber and the farmers, put the empty glasses on the bar and signalled to the barman to fill them up.

He and Mr Bamber both had their backs to me, so I only realized they were talking together because Gregory was listening. His head was raised and one ear was cocked. His eyes were on Mr Bamber. Maybe he was looking for the mobile phone.

I told myself not to jump to conclusions.

"Don't jump to conclusions," I said. "There's nothing suspicious about two men speaking to each other while they're standing next to each other at a bar."

And then the barman put the drinks down and the man picked them up and turned round.

There could be something suspicious about two men speaking to each other while they're standing at a bar if one of the men is Mr Bamber, property developer, and the other is Barry Ludgate, plumber and son of Caroline.

I threw myself to the ground before Barry could see me.

I was relieved and shocked at the same time. Relieved because the informer wasn't one of the Greeners, and shocked because it was Caroline Ludgate's own son. Maybe he'd never forgiven her for leaving him at the shopping centre.

It was up to me to do something. Sherlock Holmes would have put on some brilliant disguise, strolled into the pub and joined their conversation. But even if I'd had a brilliant disguise ready, it would have needed to make me a lot taller to even get me into the pub without being shouted at to leave the second I stepped inside.

I was still trying to work out some plan of action when the pub door opened and Mr Bamber and Gregory stepped out. They walked down the path a bit, but then Mr Bamber stopped and started punching numbers into his mobile.

I held my breath.

"It's Bamber," said Mr Bamber. "There's been a change of plan. Have everything ready to go on Sunday."

111

Gregory, who had reached the road without realizing that he was on his own, started walking back the way he and Mr Bamber had come.

"Gregory!" shouted Mr Bamber. "Gregory! Heel!"

Gregory kept walking.

Mr Bamber started to follow. "Look," he shouted into the mobile, "I've got to catch the dog. Make sure you've got it straight. We start work on Sunday, not Monday. Got it? Sunday. Crack of dawn."

I was stunned. After Mr Bamber and Gregory had disappeared from view, I started walking in a daze in the direction we'd been going before Mr Bamber went into the pub. There was a full moon, but it was a cloudy night and the moon kept vanishing. I walked and walked, trying to make out landmarks in the shadows of the night. It was when what I thought was the stone wall that ran alongside Mr Meadows' farm turned out, on closer inspection, to be a hedgerow, that I knew I was lost.

I know our area a lot better than I know the palm of my hand. If you showed me a print of my palm I wouldn't know it was mine, but if you showed me a photograph of any road within a five mile radius of my house I'd recognize it immediately. Assuming the photograph was taken in daylight. But at night it was too dark to see anything clearly.

112

"Oh, no…" I groaned out loud. I had no idea where I was.

I wanted to join the Boy Scouts when all the other boys in my class did, but my mother wouldn't let me, of course. She said the Boy Scouts was a paramilitary organization with a dodgy past and that no son of hers was going to be part of it. "Next thing you know, you'll want to join the SAS," said my mother.

So I had no Boy Scout skills to rely on. I didn't even have a torch. Sherlock Holmes was never a Boy Scout either, but he would have had a torch with him. Or at least a box of matches.

I decided to keep going until I either came to a phonebox or worked out where I was.

I was thinking of what I'd tell my parents when I rang them to come and get me when the road was suddenly lit up. All I could see were two headlights coming towards me. I moved over and turned my head away.

Much to my horror the car was stopping.

"I don't believe this," I muttered to myself. "Now I have strangers offering me lifts."

I knew what happened to people who took lifts from strangers. My grandmother was always showing me newspaper articles about people who were last seen getting into an unknown car. People who took lifts from strangers ended up in ditches or buried in shallow graves.

113

I was much too young to die. Acting on instinct, I hurled myself into the shadows at the side of the road.

The back door opened. A circle of blue light hovered in the darkness and an all too familiar voice called out, "Be careful, Elmo. Those are nettles!"

As if I hadn't worked that out already.

Mrs Bamber's head poked out of the window on the driver's side. "Elmo Blue, what are you doing out here at this time of night?"

With a great deal of pain, I freed myself from the nettles and limped to the car.

"I went for a walk," I explained to Mrs Bamber as I climbed into the back next to Kuba. "I suppose I got lost."

"Well, thank goodness we came this way," said Mrs Bamber. "Kuba wanted to go for a little drive. See the area a bit."

Mrs Bamber started humming along with the radio once we were moving.

Kuba looked at me out of the corner of her eye.

"Did you see Barry Ludgate?" she whispered.

I nodded. I was too tired to be surprised.

"There's been a change of plan," I whispered back. "They're starting the destruction on Sunday, not Monday."

"Isn't my father clever." Kuba smiled. "That's so they can start without the Greeners getting in the way. We should have known he'd never give your mother the chance to get the whole country involved."

"So what do we do now?" I wasn't actually asking, I was just wondering out loud.

"We stop him," said Kuba. "What else can we do?"

I have to say that I wasn't too keen on the idea of lying down in the mud. "You mean we're going to block the bulldozers, too?"

"Not *we*," said Kuba. "I can't interfere, remember? You'll have to stop them."

She said it as though she were saying something perfectly logical, possible and reasonable, like "You'll have to go to the shops".

"But I'm just a kid."

"You won't exactly be alone," said Kuba. "I'll be with you." She grinned. "At least, in spirit."

"Oh, great," I said. "Everything's all right then, isn't it?"

MR BAMBER AND QUITE A FEW OTHER PEOPLE GET A SURPRISE

The Greeners spent Saturday night in our living-room, finalizing their plans for Monday morning for the umpteenth time. My mother called every television and radio station that might be interested in the story, and every newspaper, too. On Monday morning the road to the woods would be chock-a-block with Greeners, cameramen, police and reporters – just as she wanted.

The only thing that wouldn't be there, of course, was whatever Mr Bamber's bulldozers had levelled the day before.

I spent Saturday night watching Mr Bamber on my computer as he finalized his plans for Sunday morning. It was Kuba's idea. I did learn some useful information – like what time the bulldozers were starting – but apart from that it wasn't really very interesting for the first few hours. Mr Bamber was on the phone all the time. Mrs Bamber kept walking in and out of any room he was in, glaring at him, but he didn't pay much attention.

"Not now, Arabella," he'd hiss whenever she tried to interrupt him. "Can't you see I'm busy?"

When Mr Bamber did finally hang up, Mrs Bamber was waiting for him. He turned off his phone and she marched into the room. That's when it started to get interesting.

"When aren't you busy?" demanded Mrs Bamber. "You never have time for anything else any more. You're like a man obsessed."

"It'll all be over tomorrow," said Mr Bamber calmly. "Then things will get back to normal."

"No they won't," said Mrs Bamber. "It's never over. You think normal is a meeting or you with a phone glued to your ear. After these houses there'll be others. There'll be shopping centres and industrial estates..."

Mr Bamber didn't look like he thought this would be too much of a disaster. He smiled.

"You don't mind driving the Porsche, Arabella. You don't mind the expensive house and the nice clothes."

"Never mind all that," snapped Mrs Bamber. "What about Kuba?"

At the mention of her name, Kuba – who, on the grounds that she couldn't directly interfere, was ignoring the Bambers and was putting one of my jigsaw puzzles together in record time – looked up.

"You hardly talk to the child," Mrs Bamber was saying. "We haven't done one family thing together since she arrived."

"She was meant to be a boy," answered Mr Bamber. He seemed to think this was an explanation.

"She was meant to be a *child*," said Mrs Bamber. "And don't give me that 'I wanted a son' malarkey. You only wanted a son so you could get a spy inside Grace Blue's house."

Kuba's head appeared at my shoulder.

"You know, I think she really cares," said Kuba. She grinned at the image on the screen. "Go for it, Mum," she urged.

As if she'd heard her, Mrs Bamber went for it.

"She might as well be a rock for all the attention you've given her." Mrs Bamber had been more or less whispering so as not to wake the child she thought was sleeping upstairs, but now she stepped up the volume. "Maybe if she had headlights and could mow things down you'd give her some of your precious time."

Mr Bamber sighed wearily.

"Arabella, please … as soon as this is over, I promise we'll do something as a family. Go to Disneyland or something."

Kuba snorted. "If he doesn't watch it, we'll all be going to jail."

                    *   *   *

It was still dark when I got up on Sunday morning and tiptoed from the house. With a stealth worthy of Holmes himself, I tiptoed to the garage and got my bike. Kuba was waiting at the end of the road.

"What happened to you?" she demanded. "Your eyes are the size of currants. You look like you've been sitting in front of a computer for the past twenty-four hours."

I didn't feel like that. I felt as though I'd been wrestling alien monsters.

"I didn't sleep very much."

Which was something of an understatement. All night I'd been dozing for an hour or so, and then waking up with this cold feeling of dread. I was more than a little nervous about standing up to the chainsaws and the bulldozers. Maybe my mother was right after all, and it would be better to keep the woods and the lake and everything else rather than build another development, but progress was progress. You couldn't stop progress. And you could get hurt if you tried. What if something went wrong and I was tragically run over?

Kuba, in contrast, was what my grandmother would have described as "bright-eyed and bushy-tailed". In the last hour of darkness, she almost seemed to glow.

"There's nothing to worry about," Kuba assured me. "The bulldozers aren't going to be turned on a little boy."

It was easy for her to say.

I said, "Um..."

Being mowed down wasn't my only worry. It had occurred to me during the night that if I did survive, everyone in Campton would hear what had happened. I'd be the laughing stock of the whole school. It was bad enough that I was the son of Grace Blue, the Green Menace. Now, for the rest of my school life I'd be Elmo Blue, Campton Secondary's representative of the lunatic fringe. I could hear Eddie Kilgour calling me imaginative names like Batbrain and Dozy, the Eighth Dwarf. It might be better if I was tragically killed; at least I'd get some sympathy.

Kuba didn't push it.

"Did you leave the note for your mum?" she asked.

The note told my mother where I was and what I was doing, and asked her to hurry. I was more likely to forget my name than forget to leave that.

"I put it on the kettle." That way I was sure she'd see it. She always had a cup of tea first thing.

"I left a note for Mrs Bamber, too," said Kuba. "I wouldn't want her to find me gone and start to worry."

If you asked me, Mrs Bamber didn't have anything to worry about. For one thing, Kuba was already dead.

"I see you've got the sign." Kuba pointed to the large square of white card with the words *SAVE OUR WOODS* in large green letters that I had under my arm. "Have you got the handcuffs?"

The handcuffs, like the sign, belonged to the Greeners and would enable me to chain myself to a handy bulldozer if I had to.

"They're in my pocket."

Kuba climbed on to the crossbar of my bike.

"Right," she said. "All systems go."

"Are you sure you know where we're going?"

Kuba looked down at me from her perch on the crossbar. "Yes, I'm sure." She patted her jacket pocket. "I've got Mr Bamber's map of the development in my pocket. I know exactly where the bulldozers will start."

"You *stole* Mr Bamber's map?" I nearly steered us off the road, I was so surprised. "I thought you weren't meant to interfere."

"I didn't steal it, I borrowed it," said Kuba. "Borrowing Mr Bamber's map is not interfering. If, unbeknownst to Mr Bamber, I changed the map, then that would be interfering."

"You sound more like a politician than an angel," I said acidly. There was enough light now for her to see the scornful expression on my face.

But Kuba didn't hear the acid in my voice or

see the scorn on my face.

"Stop over there!" she directed. "We've got to walk the rest of the way. But first we'd better have a look at the map."

Mr Bamber's map was an Ordnance Survey map, but more than that – it was Mr Bamber's battle plan. The land to be used for the development was highlighted in green.

"I think that's his idea of a joke," said Kuba.

Dark orange circles marked the routes and positions of the bulldozers.

"Well," I said. "I think the quickest way is through the graveyard."

The road the bulldozers would be coming along was on the other side. When they reached the field behind the cemetery the road forked left and right. They would surround Mr Bamber's land and attack it from three directions.

We hid the bike and started walking through the graveyard.

I'd been in the woods, through the old cemetery and even on the lake dozens of times, but I'd never been in any of those places at five in the morning before. Not just the cemetery, but the woods themselves looked really spooky. There was a heavy mist that made the light almost sparkle. Shadows wove through it like mythical creatures that vanish with the sun.

"You can see why people used to believe in ghosts and fairies," I whispered.

"And angels," said Kuba.

I shivered as I followed Kuba between the carved stones. Even though the sun was breaking, it was cold.

We finally got to the edge of the field.

I peered into the gloom. Tiny lights shimmered towards us on the road straight ahead.

"That's not a bulldozer," I said uneasily. "That's a car."

I didn't remember any mention of cars.

"Security guards," said Kuba calmly.

"Security guards?" I didn't remember any mention of security guards either. "What security guards?"

Kuba gave me a scathing look. "You didn't expect Mr Bamber to send in the chainsaws and bulldozers without protecting them, did you? Just in case?"

Now I didn't just have to worry about being squashed, I also had to worry about being shot.

"So now what am I meant to do?" I groaned. "The security guards will have me before I get anywhere near the bulldozers."

"Stop panicking," she ordered. "I'm here, aren't I? You'll be fine."

"Oh, right," I grumbled. "My guardian angel."

Only Kuba wasn't right there, was she? I was in the middle of the road, holding my placard, and Kuba Bamber was nowhere in sight.

"Just block the fork so they can't turn without running you over," she'd ordered. "And if they do grab you, try to handcuff yourself to their car."

The lights were getting closer and closer, but I didn't know what to do.

That is, I *knew* what to do. I'd seen Grace Blue lie down in front of a bulldozer on the news. And so had Eddie Kilgour. He'd tortured me for months with that one. "Is your mother still throwing herself in front of cars?" he'd call when he passed me in the hall. When it was the school cake sale he'd suggested that my mother bring the road pizza. But that was in primary school. I'd been hoping that secondary school would be different. There were so many new kids – kids who didn't know anything about me or my family – that I finally had a chance to be treated like a human being and not a geek.

I just didn't know if I could do it. I wondered if my mother had found my note yet. She and Gertie always got up really early. My mother, being a gardener, didn't like to waste any daylight, and Gertie, being a baby, woke up with the sun. My mother might already be on her way with the Press. I crossed my fingers. I could only hope that she wasn't bringing the milk float.

The security car arrived first. There were two lorries and six bulldozers behind it.

Instinct must have taken over again because I immediately sat down. I raised my placard high.

There were three large men in the car. The one who was driving stopped a few feet away from me and got out.

He was even larger out of the car than he had been in it.

He gave me this big fake smile.

"Hello there, young fellow," he said as if he was practising to be Father Christmas or something. "And what are you doing out here all by yourself at this hour of the morning?"

I moved my sign towards him in case he hadn't read the message.

"I'm stopping you from clearing the woods."

He kept smiling.

"Why don't you go home, little boy? Your mother will be worried if she finds you're not there."

"My mother would be here too if Mr Bamber hadn't lied about when he was starting to clear the woods," I said very loudly.

The other two guards had also got out of the car by now. One of them sort of smirked.

"It must be the Green Menace's boy," he said with a wink at me. "Did your mother put you up to this?"

"No." I was amazed at how calm I sounded. "My mother didn't put me up to this."

The man driving the first lorry leaned out of his cab.

"What's going on?" he yelled.

"We'll just be a minute," said the first security guard. Still smiling as if he was going to fall over with happiness, he started towards me. "Why don't you get out of the way before you get hurt, lad?"

"Why don't *you* get out of the way before *you* get hurt?" I asked back. It was really scary: I sounded just like Grace Blue.

I was holding the sign so tightly that my hands ached. The security guard took another step towards me.

"Because I'm bigger than you, that's why," he informed me.

And then I started to sound even more like Grace Blue.

"Might does not mean right," I told him.

This isn't a quote from the Bible, as far as I know. It's a quote from my mother. It's what she always says when other people tell her that you can't fight the town hall. I'd never really understood what it meant before, but sitting there with the guard bearing down on me I suddenly understood it completely. It meant that having the money and power to do something didn't make it the right thing to do. And it also meant that not having money and power didn't make you wrong, or mean that you couldn't stand up for what was right. Up

126

till now I'd been doing what Kuba pushed me into doing – and because I'd seen my mother crying on the computer that time. But suddenly I really was there because I wanted to be. I was in the right; I knew I was. I held my sign even higher.

All the men were laughing, even the ones in the bulldozers.

"Might doesn't make right..." The first security guard was practically doubled up and choking. "Now I've heard everything."

"Not quite," said a pleasant voice behind me.

I glanced over my shoulder.

The guard scowled at Kuba. "Where did you come from?"

"From that field over there." She jerked her head towards the field next to the cemetery. "I was going for a walk."

The guard turned his scowl on me. "Is this girl a friend of yours?"

I nodded. "Yeah," I reluctantly admitted. "She's a friend of mine."

Kuba sat down at the edge of the road to my right, out of the way but in view. I assumed this was her idea of non-interference.

I must admit that it surprised me, but I was glad to see her. On the other hand, she didn't make me feel less nervous. I really didn't want her to do something she wasn't supposed to do. It was bad enough being in trouble with the law without being in trouble with God as well.

"What *are* you doing here?" I hissed. "You're not supposed to—"

The rest of my sentence never reached my lips because I suddenly noticed the men. They were staring past us, their eyes wide with horror. They looked sort of green and they were walking backwards.

I turned round to see what they were staring at.

Hundreds of people were walking towards us from the top of the field. I thought at first that they were the armies of the Greeners. I searched the crowd for my mother. She should have been right at the front.

She wasn't at the front, though. Which wasn't the only thing that made me think they weren't the Greeners after all.

The people coming through the field were all dressed up, but not one of them was wearing a coat. The women were in long skirts and big hats, and the men were all in suits. There were tons of children with them. That surprised me, because of the time of day. If they weren't Greeners, the adults could have been on their way home from a very big costume party, but it was a bit early for children's parties. The girls were in starched yellow-white dresses and most of the boys wore whitish suits. There were a few cats and dogs walking with them. One woman even had a budgie. It was strange because, although they were a crowd, you could tell that they weren't together. I'd been on a couple of demonstrations with my mother and everybody always chatted as they walked along. But although some of these people were talking, they weren't talking to each other, they were talking to themselves. And they were laughing and crying to themselves, too. None of them looked like they'd seen daylight for a while.

"What's this, then?" demanded the first security guard. His voice wobbled. You could hear the fear.

I turned back to him. He wasn't so tough any more. His face was the white of ashes, and so were the faces of the other men.

"Tell them to stop!" ordered one of the guards. He was moving backwards towards the car door. "Tell them to stop!"

"Stop," said Kuba.

The people kept coming, their eyes on the car and the men who were now pushing each other to get inside it first.

"They won't stop!" called Kuba as doors slammed shut and the mob of men, women, children and animals passed us like a cloud. "I've tried, but they won't stop."

The car backed up so fast it hit the first lorry.

I turned to Kuba.

"Who *are* all these people?" I whispered.

Kuba's smile was like a fire on a stormy night.

"I can't interfere," said Kuba, "but I am allowed to raise the dead."

Mrs Bamber and my mother arrived next. They were in the silver Porsche. My mother was clutching the petitions and Mrs Bamber was leaning on the horn. They were both wearing their dressing-gowns – in my mother's case an old pink terry-towelling bathrobe with baby vomit stains all down the front, in Mrs Bamber's something shining and silver.

The last of the dead were just melting into the air, mingling with the dust and fumes of the car, lorries and bulldozers as they made their escape. It reminded me of the earlier mist.

The driver of the first bulldozer had forced himself into the car with the guards, leaving the bulldozer sitting in the road. Mrs Bamber drove around it as if it were a piece of tyre on the motorway.

My mother and Mrs Bamber were out of the Porsche faster than you could say, "Keep our planet green".

"Kuba!" Mrs Bamber was practically in tears. "Kuba, I've been worried sick. Are you all right?"

My mother was not practically in tears, she's a tougher sort than Mrs Bamber, but she

130

did scoop me up in her arms with a, "What a brave boy."

I was glad none of the men were there to see it, even though I hugged her back.

In answer to Mrs Bamber's question, Kuba said, "Yes, I'm fine. I went for a walk with Elmo."

Mrs Bamber was still sobbing and telling Kuba never to do a thing like that again when my father and Mr Bamber showed up. My father had Gertie in a kind of rucksack on his back and was riding his bicycle. Mr Bamber was in the BMW. He was talking on his mobile and he looked pretty annoyed. Gregory was beside him.

My father threw his bike down. Gertie waved.

"Thank God you're all right," gasped my father.

I didn't look at Kuba.

Gregory wouldn't get out of the car, but Mr Bamber charged out like a wild animal whose cage door was suddenly opened.

He stopped when he saw Mrs Bamber. He wasn't expecting her.

"Arabella! What on earth are you doing here?"

Not that he gave her a chance to answer.

"I had a call from my guards. Some non-sense about zombies—" He broke off as if he'd only just noticed the rest of us. Especially my mother. He used quite a few words I'm not allowed to use myself, but basically what he wanted to know was what was going on.

My mother told him. She said Mrs Bamber had woken up early and gone into Kuba's room to check on her. Kuba hadn't been there, but she'd found Kuba's note saying that she was with me. Mrs Bamber had raced across the road and banged on the kitchen door. My mother had been up and just finishing reading the note I'd left her.

"Apparently Elmo thought you might try something like this," my mother finished, "so he came to stop you."

Mr Bamber looked like he had plenty left to say himself, but before he could get over his surprise that it was I who'd turned back the bulldozers, two police cars, a Range Rover and a red Ford all screeched to a halt behind the BMW, which was behind the bulldozer.

My father looked at my mother.

"I rang the police and the papers before we set off," said my mother.

Mr Bamber said a few words about what he thought about that.

A flash went off as my mother stuck the petitions into his arms.

SOMEDAY THE TRUE STORY MAY BE TOLD

There wasn't a newspaper in the country that didn't have at least one article about the Battle of Campton. Not so much because they agreed that might didn't mean right, but because of the interesting twist in the story. In their interviews, the security guards and bulldozer drivers all mentioned the hordes of people who came towards them across the field. Some of the papers called the hordes people, but others called them "apparitions" or "zombies" or "the living dead". Some of the papers suggested that the people were just Greeners, dressed up to shock.

My mother was happy to let them think that.

"If you ask me," said my mother, "those idiots made up the zombies so they wouldn't look even more foolish, being frightened away by a small boy."

Personally, I didn't think she had to say "small".

The photo they ran in the papers of Mr Bamber showed him smiling good-naturedly. The caption underneath quoted him as saying that the Greeners had won "fair and square". "A good businessman listens to the voice of the people," said Mr David Bamber.

Because of all the publicity, the Council gave in to public opinion. Not only did they refuse Mr Bamber his permission, they declared the woods, the churchyard and the lake a historic area.

"Better late than never," said my father.

Mrs Bamber and Kuba were not only invited to the Greeners' victory party, they actually came. Mrs Bamber brought champagne from her husband's wine cellar.

"He'll be furious when he finds out," she said cheerfully. "But since he's already furious…"

Across the road, I could see Mr Bamber and Gregory looking out of the living-room window. Gregory almost looked as if he wanted to come to the party. Mr Bamber was glaring.

He may have been publicly defeated, but privately he vowed that he wasn't going to give up just because of one minor setback. "There's plenty more land where that came from," is what he said at home.

"He says I'm not allowed to play with Elmo

any more," said Kuba. "He doesn't even want me to talk to him."

"I can live with that," I said.

Everybody thought I was joking.

"David wanted me to keep the curtains permanently closed in the front room," Mrs Bamber told my mother. "So he wouldn't have to be reminded all the time."

My mother had obviously forgotten that she had once wanted to board up our front window so she wouldn't see Mr Bamber. She laughed.

"How childish," said my mother. "What did you say?"

"I sent the curtains to the cleaners," said Mrs Bamber. "I only stopped him from putting the house up for sale by threatening to leave him."

"He is a stubborn man, isn't he?" said Grace Blue.

"Well, he met his Waterloo this time," said my father.

"Actually, it's the Alamo," said Mrs Bamber, Kuba and I all at once.

Nobody noticed. My mother had wrenched the cork from a bottle of champagne and was spilling it into glasses, although most of it went on the floor.

"I think this calls for a toast," said my mother when everyone but Kuba, me and Gertie had a glass. "To Elmo Eugene Sheriff

Blue!" she cried.

Beside me, Kuba snorted.

"And Ku—" My mother smiled at Kuba. "That can't be your full name..."

"It isn't my name at all," said Kuba, but she didn't sound bothered. "My full name is Kulliana Nieves Isabella Verde."

"It was as close as we could get," murmured Mrs Bamber.

"Doesn't 'Verde' mean green?" asked my mother.

"Yes," said Kuba, "yes, it does."

"Well, what a coincidence," said my mother. She looked at the rest of us. "Isn't that quite a coincidence? We're the Blues, and I belong to the Greeners..."

I was the only one who didn't say what an amazing coincidence it was.

I looked over at Kuba. She was smiling and nodding as if she'd never come across a coincidence like that before.

"So what happens now?" I whispered. "Do you just disappear?"

"Disappear?" She took a sip of her drink. We had fresh apple juice, of course. "Why would I do that?"

I didn't like her tone.

"Because you've accomplished your mission," I said calmly. "Your job here is done."

"To Elmo Blue and Kuba Green!" my mother was shouting.

Kuba clinked her glass against mine.

"My job's not done," said Kuba. "My job here has only just begun."

UNDERCOVER ANGEL STRIKES AGAIN
Dyan Sheldon

Elmo Blue's neighbour Kuba is a little angel. Literally.

But she's making Elmo's life more like hell than heaven. All he wants to do is fit in, but Kuba has other ideas… When the class goes on a history trip to a remote part of Wales, Elmo, thanks to Kuba, finds himself embroiled in a war against bully Eddie Kilgour and his side-kick Mark. It looks as though Elmo himself could be history, unless he gets some miraculous help.

"A hilarious fantasy."
International Board on Books for Young People

DANDELION & BOBCAT
Veronica Bennett

Bobcat doesn't want a foster-sister – especially not one like Dandelion…

Not only does she have the weirdest looks he's ever seen, but she tells all his classmates that her real mother has been kidnapped! Bobcat doesn't know if she's lying or just plain nuts, but some unexplained events make him wonder if there is more to Dandelion than meets the eye. Why do her crazy predictions keep coming true? Who are her real parents? And do the answers lie in the mysterious Tarantula computer game?

Fast-paced, funny and sprinkled with magic, this is a hugely enjoyable story from the author of *Monkey*.

CONFESSIONS OF A
TEENAGE DRAMA QUEEN
Dyan Sheldon

Mary Elizabeth Cep (or Lola, as she prefers to be called) longs to be in the spotlight. But when she moves to New Jersey with her family, Lola discovers that the role of resident drama queen at Dellwood "Deadwood" High has already been filled – by the Born-to-Win, Born-to-Run-Everything Carla Santini. Once the curtain goes up on the school play, which drama queen will take centre stage?

"Lola will rightfully take her place among the unforgettable and lively female characters of young adult novels. Like its heroine, the story is off-beat, outrageous and utterly charming." *School Library Journal*

"High school has always been this stressful, but rarely this hilarious." *Booklist*

"Delicious reading... Home-grown drama queens and teen shrinking violets will love it." *Kids Out*

Now a major feature film starring Lindsay Lohan!